NANCY WARREN

STOCKINGS AND SPELLS

VAMPIRE KNITTING CLUB
BOOK FOUR

INTRODUCTION

A Holiday Market
With crafts, toys, hot chocolate
And a killer!

The Vampire Knitting Club decide to take part in Oxford's Holiday Market, selling exquisite hand knit scarves, sweaters and gift items. Their most popular item is the hand knitted Christmas stocking, brightly colored and extra long to squeeze in a few extra small gifts.

But when a sales clerk in another booth is found strangled with one of the stockings, Lucy Swift and her undead detectives are on the case, determined to find out who would do such a terrible thing. And why.

Life at Cardinal Woolsey's knitting shop, in Oxford, England, is as colorful as the most garish Christmas sweater.

The best way to keep up with new releases and special offers is to join Nancy's newsletter at **nancywarren.net.**

STOCKINGS AND SPELLS

CHAPTER 1

The December day dawned bright, or as bright as a day can dawn in Oxford, England, in December—which is to say, not very. Winters in our part of Oxfordshire were cloudy and cold which was, no doubt, why so many vampires chose to live here. Between the network of tunnels that ran underneath the city, and the number of cloudy days, they rarely had to worry about the sun.

Winter was when my vampire knitting club was happiest.

I was dressed nearly head-to-toe in garments hand-knitted by my undead friends. On my head was a stylish red cloche hat that kept my ears warm, circling my neck was a red and blue scarf featuring a complicated geometric pattern and on my hands were matching mittens. I'd bought my navy blue coat, but beneath it I wore a gorgeous knitted dress. Even my black stockings were done by hand, though I think that was mainly Sylvia showing off.

My high-heeled boots tapped over the cobblestones in front of Cardinal College on Harrington Street. There weren't many students hanging around on the frozen-crisp grass, they were all inside, presumably at lectures or studying somewhere warm.

I dodged a few ambling shoppers as I hurried to Cardinal Woolsey's, the knitting and yarn shop that I inherited when my grandmother died. Or, sort of died, as she was now an enthusiastic member of the vampire knitting club.

I'd left my new assistant in charge of the shop while I went across the street to Frogg's Books where I'd put in an order. After puzzling over Christmas gifts for vampires who owned everything they could possibly want, I'd settled on newly-released books.

I didn't like to leave my assistant alone in the shop for too long. Her name was Meritamun and she was an Egyptian witch who'd been trapped in a cursed mirror for three millennia. As a result, she had missed a lot of developments in the world. She was convinced, for example, that everything operated by electricity actually had a spirit trapped within it. I'd caught her trying to release a spirit from the microwave just last week. I'd been popping corn and she'd become so convinced the tiny explosions were the witch banging on the door to be let out that she'd magicked the door open.

I was still finding stray kernels of popped corn, like little ghosts, hiding in the dish drainer, the cutlery drawer and under the fridge. At least Nyx, my black cat, had enjoyed the experience. She'd decided that microwave popcorn was a cat toy in disguise.

Meri was deeply suspicious of the cash register in Cardinal Woolsey's, and the electric lights, but otherwise it was a pretty old-fashioned place. She couldn't knit, but then, neither could I. We were both taking lessons from the vampires. I'd hired Meri as my assistant because she had nowhere else to go. However, now that we'd been working together for a few weeks, I'd grown extremely fond of her.

She was always patient. I suppose being stuck in a mirror for three thousand years would teach patience. She loved the color and texture of wool. I really thought she was happiest sitting quietly with her knitting. With the modern world being so loud and confusing, I could understand that.

Unfortunately, December was a busy month at Cardinal Woolsey's as knitters rushed in to pick up the supplies they'd need for their gift lists. I was surprised that knitting had so many procrastinators. I suspected there would be many a pair of knitting needles clacking together into the wee hours of Christmas morning.

As I approached my little shop, warm satisfaction washed over me. The front window brimmed with a colorful display of sweater kits—appropriate as a gift for the knitter or as a project to be hastily completed by Christmas. There was an array of snuggly sweaters for those without the time or inclination to actually knit something. My favorite part of the display was the four hand-knitted Christmas stockings hanging in front of a painted fireplace complete with licking orange flames. The artwork was courtesy of Theodore, one of the vampire knitters, who, apart from being a former policeman, had painted sets for amateur theater productions. And, curled up in front of the fire, almost as though she could feel the warmth, was my black cat, and familiar, Nyx.

I'd put twinkly lights all around the window and the painted fireplace so my shop looked festive and inviting.

When I walked in, the place was bustling. Meri was trapped in the corner with a young, intense man. As the door closed behind me, she sent me a glance of appeal, and I went straight over, ignoring three other customers who all seemed to be browsing. Before I could ask how I could help, the guy turned to me. "I'm looking for a knitted iPad cover and she says she doesn't know what I'm talking about. An iPad cover. How complicated is that?"

Of course, I'd talked to Meri about computers in general, but we hadn't had time to go through every permutation from the smartphone to the tablet. I smiled, soothingly. "I'm afraid we don't have any knitted iPad covers, or any patterns to make them. It's a good idea, though."

Now, he looked even more annoyed. "Why couldn't she just tell me that?"

"She's from Egypt," I said, as though that explained everything.

He shook his head. "I think they have iPads in Egypt."

Not in the middle Kingdom.

After that very dissatisfied customer had stalked out, I turned to Meri, who looked flustered and anxious. "Don't worry. You're catching on really fast."

She nodded, gratefully, and headed to the cash desk where a customer had a sweater kit and a knitting pattern book she wanted to buy. It would be a nice, smooth, easy purchase, exactly what Meri needed to get her confidence back.

She might not be a knitting genius, or conversant with every kind of computer on the planet, but Meri was surprisingly good with customers. She'd been a servant to a lesser wife of one of the pharaohs, so she was used to serving, and she did it well. When she'd finished with the customer, she came to me with the notebook she always carried. In it, she'd write questions for me, or reminders of things she'd learned.

She had a good memory and listened intently, so I knew she'd catch on eventually, she just had a lot of catching up to do.

It wasn't always easy, as Meri lived in my guest room upstairs and we worked together. However, she was a much more experienced witch than I was, so, while I could help her to navigate the modern world, she was trying to help me settle into being a witch.

We were busy for the rest of the day, and afterwards we went upstairs to the flat above the shop. For our dinner I'd bought kebabs and was making a spiced rice dish I'd found online. I tried to cook things that would be familiar to Meri, or at least not make her turn away in horror as she had the first time she saw black pudding. After dinner, she read the local newspaper as she liked to know what was going on and she could ask me about anything that was confusing. Which was quite a bit.

Since the vampire knitting club was meeting that night, I decided to stay in and practice my own knitting. Even though my former assistant, Eileen, had turned out to be a soul-sucking demon, she had helped me improve my knitting. She got me to begin with a simple square. I was on my third square now and one of these days I was going to complete a square that didn't look as though it had been attacked by moths. Or hungry lions. Or turned into every geometric shape *but* square. I don't know how I dropped so many stitches and why I could never find them. I think even the endless patience of the vampires was beginning to run thin.

The buzzer on the house phone went off about eight o'clock that night, indicating there was someone at the door. It was my grandmother and her best friend and maker,

5

Sylvia. They came in both wearing smart new outfits. Sylvia, who in life had been a stage and screen star in the 1920s, always looked glamorous. But my grandmother always looked like a quintessential grandmother. And she still did. She wore her white hair coiled neatly in a bun, her lined face was as kind as ever, but I was pretty sure that if I looked inside her coat, I would see a designer's name on the label.

"How was your trip?" I asked, holding out my arms. I hugged first my grandmother, and then Sylvia. "I didn't expect you back so soon."

Gran hadn't had much chance to travel in life. She'd been widowed young and had run Cardinal Woolsey's for more than fifty years. Now that she was undead, she had the time and some very rich friends who also liked to travel. She and Sylvia had been in Paris and Rome.

They were full of news. "We had the most wonderful time. The shopping there is simply amazing. And vampires there don't have a friendly knitting shop like we do. We really think it's time for you to expand. Start a franchise."

I shook my head. "I appreciate that you'd like to attend vampire knitting club meetings whenever you travel, but I can barely manage one shop. I don't think I'm ready for more."

They glanced at each other as though my response was exactly what they'd expected. Gran patted my hand. "Just think about it."

I felt that there was more coming but for now they let it be.

I took their coats, and a quick peek confirmed that Gran was indeed shopping the designers these days. Then, we all settled in the living room on the chintz chairs and the comfy couch. Sylvia turned to Meri, who'd already moved on from single-colored squares and was knitting a scarf. Her stitches were more fluid and even than mine. I tried not to be jealous. With all she'd been through, I should be happy she was enjoying knitting. "How are you getting along, dear?"

Meri was not one to blow her own horn. She cast her eyes down to the floor and said, "Lucy is very patient with me. I make so many mistakes. There is much I do not understand."

"She's doing a wonderful job," I said. "And, as soon as she is more used to this millennium, she'll be an incredible assistant."

It was not lost on me that the assistants I'd hired had turned out to be disasters, while the one I'd freed from a cursed mirror, turned out to be the best choice.

"And how was Samhain?" Gran wanted to know.

I'd finally gone to one of the coven's events which took place at a circle of ancient standing stones not far from Moreton-Under-Wychwood. "Fine," I said airily. Gran would find out soon enough what a disaster my first witch social gathering had been, but I didn't have the heart to tell her quite yet. Instead, I changed the subject back to what they'd seen on their travels. A much safer topic. I wished I was a powerful enough witch that I could erase the evening from the memories of all who'd been there that night.

At ten o'clock, the four of us went downstairs to join the vampire knitting club in the back room of my shop. About fifteen vampires showed up, either coming up through the trapdoor from their underground apartment complex, which was accessed through the tunnel that ran under my shop, or walking in through the shop door. They were happy to see Sylvia and Gran and, after everyone was settled and the knitting needles were flying at warp speed, the crochet hooks travelling so fast they looked like tiny firework displays, I settled to my own knitting. These knitters, who had been practicing their craft for hundreds of years, would put any modern knitter to shame. Still, they very kindly encouraged me, and I kept trying.

We always chatted and gossiped while we worked, but I could feel a strange suppressed energy in the group. I had a feeling they had something on their collective minds, but, I decided not to ask. Probably, whatever it was, I didn't want to know.

We knitted on.

Finally, Alfred said, "Lucy? There's something we want to discuss with you."

Yep, here it came. I'd seen them glancing amongst themselves and clearly Alfred had been nominated to bring up whatever subject they were keen to discuss. "What is it?" I asked.

"We've been thinking, we'd like to have a booth at the Oxford holiday market, this year."

I was so surprised, I dropped my knitting. I think a stitch or two came off the needle but I couldn't worry about that now. I picked up my square. For some reason, it looked like a bent triangle, something like a taco chip in shape. I glanced around at all the eager faces looking at me. "You want to do what?"

Alfred chuckled. "I thought you'd be surprised." He held up his hand, like a magician about to pull a rabbit out of a hat. "Think about it. We have so many knitted garments piling up, we need to get rid of some of them. Also, look how popular our knitted Christmas stockings have been. We've got plenty of goods to stock one of those nice little chalets in the center of town."

"But who's going to sell the stuff?" I asked.

He looked at me as though I were stupid. "We will, of course."

I don't know why I thought this was a terrible idea, but I thought it was a terrible idea. The vampires stayed out of sight, slipped quietly through this ancient city in the shadows. The Oxford holiday market brought shoppers from far and wide and they'd be in the middle of town.

I looked around. "Have you ever been to one of these markets? Do you know how crowded they get?" I didn't want to bring up the notion that all that hot pulsing blood so close to them might be too much of a temptation. They lived off a private blood bank, but I had to assume that it tasted better fresh. Plus, didn't they have an instinct to kill?

Alfred looked a little hurt, as though he'd read my mind. "We want to help."

"Help who?"

"We want to inspire people to take up handicrafts. In the time we've all roamed the earth, people have moved faster and faster, worked longer hours. Now, with modern technology, everyone is 'connected.'" He put air quotes around the word 'connected.' He shook his head. "I worry about people today. They have so much stress and so little leisure time. Knitting is relaxing, and, we'll give all the profits to charity."

I knew that every generation pretty much thought the next one was doomed. I didn't realize it worked in vampire world as well. It was sweet that they cared about the stresses of modern human life and wanted to alleviate them. Frightening, but sweet.

They could have gone ahead and got a booth without me, but, I suspected they needed my help. So, I reminded them that I was busy running my own shop.

Alfred waved that objection away. "You won't have to do anything, Lucy, just rent the booth in your name, and be the contact person."

Dr. Christopher Weaver, who ran the private blood bank, said, "And, perhaps, you could help with publicity. For instance, you could hang up our poster in your shop window."

They had a poster? "You're serious about this?" I looked around. "Does Rafe know what you're planning?"

Rafe Crosyer was their unofficial leader. I considered him a friend, but he could be very high-handed, and they would never take on an enterprise like this without his tacit permission. They all nodded in unison. "Oh yes," Alfred confirmed. "Rafe is solidly on board."

I looked at Sylvia and Gran, who had been away and, presumably, not part of the conversation. "What do you think?"

Gran smiled her sweet smile. "I think it would be lovely to be involved in a knitting shop again, even if it was only a temporary one. Though, I suppose, I wouldn't be allowed to sit in the booth and sell things."

The very idea made my skin break out in a cold sweat. Gran had been well known in this town before she passed and I had trouble as it was keeping her out of the shop in the middle of the day, when she tended to sleepwalk. We couldn't have her selling scarves at the Christmas market. People from her former life would be bound to notice.

Sylvia glanced quickly at me and then reached over and

patted Gran on her shoulder. "We'll need you to manage all the inventory, and, I know it's a lot to ask, but perhaps you could also do the accounting."

Gran, who'd looked downcast when she realized she wouldn't be on the selling floor, brightened up at the idea of being so useful. She nodded. "Yes, that's an excellent idea, Sylvia. I'd be happy to manage the back end of the enterprise."

I couldn't think of any more objections. The ones I had were vague and unformed. I wished Rafe were here, and wondered why he wasn't. Even Meri looked excited at the idea. "I have heard much about this holiday called Christmas. I look forward to seeing it with my own eyes."

I nodded. "I'll see about getting a booth. Though, we could be too late." In fact, the more I thought about it, I imagined you had to book booths months in advance.

Once more they all glanced at each other and looked sheepish. Alfred said, "Actually, you already did."

I felt my forehead wrinkle in puzzlement. "I did what?"

"You may have already made the application and filled out the forms. I believe you've already sent the committee a deposit."

I couldn't be bothered to get annoyed, what was the point? Clearly, they were using me as the front for this enterprise, and clearly I was going to let them. I rolled my eyes. "All right. Tell me what I have to do."

"You have to go tomorrow to the stallholders meeting."

"Were you planning to tell me?" If I hadn't been needed to show my face at this meeting, I wondered if they would have just gone ahead and had this knitting booth in my name, without informing me. They all spoke at once assuring me that they would never do anything I didn't like, but I wasn't too sure.

Rafe came in then. He sauntered in the front door, in spite of the fact that I had locked it. When he walked into the back room his eyes immediately sought out mine. His wintry gaze lightened. "Good evening, Lucy."

I nodded. "Hi, Rafe."

The other vampires all greeted him and then Alfred said, "We were just filling Lucy in on the details of our chalet at the holiday market."

He nodded. "You finally told her."

"We always intended to. The moment was just never right."

Rafe settled into an empty chair beside Clara, a sweet older vampire who'd been turned in the 1930s. "Have you decided on a name, yet?"

He pulled out his knitting, what looked like a sweater, made of black cashmere. It looked so soft I wanted to stroke my fingers over it. Instead, I went back to attacking my blue chunky wool.

"We're having trouble deciding on a name. I thought perhaps, Yule Knits. Clara here came up with Yuletide Treasures, Mabel suggested Christmas for Ewe."

"What do you think, Lucy?"

As long as they weren't calling themselves the Vampire Knitters any name was fine with me.

Silence Buggins, who was never one to be silent for long, said, "I think Victorian Handcrafts, would be a very nice name. No other age has been as good as mine." She simpered, "Or we could call it Silent Knits."

Sylvia rolled her eyes. "Sounds like quiet lice."

I could see a fight beginning to brew. All I needed was for them all to lay claim to why their particular era was the best. I said, before anyone else could speak, "You're all timeless. Why not Timeless Treasures?"

Sure it was probably a cliché, and there must be a million shops with a name like that, but this ragtag bunch of undead knitters were indeed timeless, and they were certainly treasures.

"I like it," Alfred said.

Clara nodded. "It has a nice ring to it."

Silence pouted for a moment, then sighed as much as her corset would allow her. "Fine."

"All right, then," I said. "I'll go to the orientation tomorrow. Is there anything else I should think about?"

Rafe said, "You might see if you can secure a chalet that's out of the path of any direct sunlight."

"Right. I'll do my best."

CHAPTER 2

I could tell that the group was excited to have a communal project. They'd always been fast knitters, but they began to turn out items with astonishing speed. I encouraged them all to make the long knitted stockings because I had a feeling they were going to be a popular item. Some of the stockings were just multicolor stripes, some decorated with buttons, others featured Santa and the reindeer, snowmen with black button eyes and red pom poms for noses, trees and stars, nativity scenes. I had to put in huge orders for wool just to keep up with them.

Sylvia and Theodore decorated the booth and decided where and how most of the products should be displayed. Naturally, I came along to help, and I think we were all pleased with the results. Theodore hand-painted the sign that said Timeless Treasures and Gran and I set the prices. We wanted them low enough to be affordable, but not so low that anyone would be suspicious of the motives of the sellers.

I stayed up extra late the night before the holiday market opened, so I could walk over with Gran and look at our booth in the middle of the night. I opened up the stall and turned on all the lights and when we stood back, it looked like a snow globe, lit up in the night. She clapped her hands. "Oh, that is so pretty."

From the first day of the Christmas market, my prediction turned out to be true. The sweaters, the scarves, the mittens and the hats were all popular, but the oversized knitted stockings were by far the most purchased items.

Since Gran couldn't be seen in the city that she'd lived and died in, and I didn't want her to feel too left out, I encouraged Silence to be Gran's deputy in keeping up production and organizing the stock. In fact, with most of the local vampires involved in the project, and no need for more than two of them in the booth at any one time, there were always going to be plenty of vampires left behind. The flat upstairs became an impromptu knitting factory, beginning in the evening when they got up and going through the night.

The market opened on the first Friday in December. I couldn't wait to close my shop and walk over to Broad Street. Meri came along, keen for yet another new experience. It was wonderful to see the historic street lit up and bustling with shoppers. When we got to Timeless Treasures, Rafe was standing outside the booth, as though he were shopping. Since he was well known as an antiquarian book expert and he taught occasional lectures at one of the colleges, he'd decided that it would look too odd if he were seen to be selling knitted goods at the market.

There were several other customers, and they weren't pretending. Two older women were picking among the extra long Christmas stockings. From how much inventory was already gone, on the first day, I could already tell the knitting booth was going to be a success.

Rafe and Alfred both greeted us, then Alfred leaned across the table and said, "Those long stockings have been selling very well, Lucy. The AB positive, over there, bought three of them," he said, pointing to a stout woman currently munching on a bag of roasted chestnuts.

"O negative, who's scowling over the wooden toys over there, dithered and said he'd think about it. Then, when he came back, the two he liked were gone."

Alfred had a sensitive digestive system. He was allergic to garlic and fussy about blood type, but even so. I eyed him with suspicion. "You're having me on. You can't smell someone's blood type in this crowd."

"Oh, can't I, Miss A Positive?"

Okay, maybe he could. "Well, make sure you stay well fed," I said in a low tone. "From the blood bank."

Rafe was chatting with Clara, but I saw him keep glancing across to the chalet facing ours, where a young woman sold handmade soaps, oils, and lotions. The sign over her booth read Bubbles. At first, I wasn't sure what he was looking at. Finally, I moved closer. "Did I get the orientation of the booth wrong?" Was he worried about the direction of the sun?

He shook his head. Glanced across again with a puzzled expression on his face. "That woman looks familiar, but I can't place her."

I looked at her more carefully. She was probably about thirty, with long, straight hair that was dyed to a copper gold color. She was pretty, with big brown eyes and a somewhat sad expression. She didn't seem to have a helper and was kept busy with a steady stream of customers. She was definitely a stranger to me. "Are you one of those people who never forgets a face?"

His eyes gleamed with humor. "In six hundred years? Trust me, I've forgotten more than a few faces."

I wondered if one day he'd forget mine, and felt a jolt of sadness.

"Maybe she was a student of yours, or her family had a book valued by you."

He shook his head. "I remember all my students. I'm sure I've never actually met her. In fact, it could simply be that she reminds me of someone."

Meri seemed fascinated by the market. I started to explain how it worked, but she stopped me with a laugh. "This reminds me of the souks at home. Many people selling wares all collected in one place."

"Exactly." It must be nice for her to see something so familiar, and low tech.

I was about to suggest that we take a tour when I looked ahead, and my heart sank.

"Double, double, toil and trouble," I muttered under my breath, watching the three witches walk toward me. If they hadn't already seen me, I'd have dived under the table to hide.

"Quoting Macbeth before dinner?" Rafe asked. "That could put you off your food."

"These three will do that all on their own." The three witches were my cousin, Violet Weeks, her grandmother, Lavinia, and a powerful witch named Margaret Twig. They came up to the booth and Margaret said, in her flat, Canadian accent, "The holiday market is booming, I see. How's business in the knitting booth?" Then she chuckled, looking from me to Rafe and back again, "My, that rhymes with kissing booth, doesn't it?"

"What do you want, Margaret?" I asked. Ms. Twig did not make social calls. Certainly not on me.

She glanced around and then lowered her voice as she leaned closer. "Just making sure you remember the Winter Solstice celebration. Yule is a very significant date on our calendar."

I couldn't believe she was suggesting I turn up for another witching event. I glanced at Violet and Lavinia to see if I was being punk'd but they both nodded as though they actually wanted me there.

"Have you forgotten what happened at Samhain?"

"Everyone has accidents, dear," my great-aunt Lavinia said soothingly.

Rafe, of course, was listening to every word. "What happened at Samhain?" he asked. "All you said was it was boring."

The three witches burst into mirth. "Boring?" Margaret Twig finally managed. "I've never been less bored."

"I'm bored now," I said with an edge. "Let's talk about something else."

But Rafe had sniffed out a good story and he wasn't going to let it drop. "Please. I'm six hundred years old. I'm so rarely surprised."

Margaret was only too happy to oblige. "On Samhain, we invited Lucy, as the newest member of our coven, to give us a little demonstration of her magic." Her sparkling blue eyes were wet with tears of laughter. "She showed us all right."

The three witches went into another frenzy of cackling. Honestly, put those three around a cauldron and they'd brew up some seriously deadly potions using nothing but their evil cackles.

Rafe merely waited, knowing she'd tell him when she had herself under control. "We were at the standing stones, you see. In fairness to Lucy, it's a very powerful area on a very powerful night. She treated us to a little display." She turned to me. "What was it you were trying to do?"

It was a spell I'd practiced and practiced. I still didn't understand how it had gone so wrong.

"I was trying to lift the hat off your head and send it home, back to the closet or drawer where you keep it." I'd been quite pleased with that spell. While practicing it, I'd managed to tidy my house and shop by magic. It seemed time efficient. Besides, I hated cleaning.

"What went wrong?" Rafe asked. I could see a slight grin trying to break out on his face in anticipation of whatever was to come.

My cousin Violet couldn't wait for Margaret. She blurted, "She uprooted one of the standing stones and sent it flying through the air."

Rafe's eyebrows rose. "Was that the UFO that several people in Oxfordshire reported seeing?"

"Yes, it was," Margaret said, glaring at Violet and taking back control of the story.

I had to explain. "Margaret, you were standing in front of the stone. My magic somehow got confused." I still wasn't certain how it had happened, but I'd been watching Margaret's hat—not a pointy witch's one, but a purple felt fedora—telling it to go back to where it had come from, when the earth trembled and a massive stone that had been rooted in that spot for millennia, shot off like a rocket and flew through the air. "And it's not funny. That stone must have weighed tons. It could have killed someone."

"In fact, it weighed nearly forty tons," Margaret said. "I know because I helped move it back."

"You found this stone?" Rafe asked.

She sent him a patronizing glance. "I'm also a powerful witch. But I can control my magic."

"Where was it?"

"The stone? About eight miles away. In a gully."

"But that information could be of geological interest. Doesn't it suggest to you that the stone returned home? That could be where it was quarried." He looked far too enthused. All I needed now was for some eager archaeologists to turn up on my doorstep.

"Can we please not turn the most humiliating night of my life into a teaching moment?"

"That is not accurate, Lucy," Meritamun said in her precise, clear voice. "You said when you found your betrothed in the act of carnal embrace with another woman that *that* was the most humiliating evening of your life." She looked genuinely puzzled. "It is not possible for two evenings to be 'the most' humiliating. One must take precedence."

I tried not to lose it on Meri. She was only trying to learn the ways, and vocabulary, of the current era. "Remind me to explain about the girlfriend code," I said to her. "Also, Cone of Silence."

Obediently, she reached for her notebook and wrote down what I'd said, for our next lesson.

"Anyway, dear," Great Aunt Lavinia said to me, "Do come to the Winter Solstice. We'll be blessing the returned stone."

She glanced at the other two witches. "Naturally, you won't be asked to do anything."

"Not even bring a shared dish for the supper afterward?" They'd told me it was customary.

They glanced among themselves. "The coven would prefer that you didn't." She glanced at Meri and said, at her most gracious, "And do bring Meritamun. She's most welcome."

I expected them to leave, having delivered the message, but they hung around for a bit, exclaiming over the stockings and pawing the merchandise. I could see Lavinia and Margaret nudging each other. Finally, Margaret straightened. "Lucy. Lavinia has a suggestion for you."

"It was your idea!"

Margaret rolled her blue cat eyes. "Fine. We think you need another assistant in your shop."

I couldn't believe my ears. She'd just mocked my attempts at spell casting and now she wanted to give me business advice? I was so stunned it took me a second to form words. I strove for politeness, so discounted anything that contained such words as None, Of, Your, and Business. I ended with, "Meri is an excellent assistant."

"Of course, she is," Lavinia said, giving Margaret the side eye. "We're a little worried, that's all, that with you having such unpredictable magic, and Meri being out of touch with modern witchery, something could happen that would negatively affect the coven."

She really said 'negatively affect' like my puny actions were up there with climate change and global election rigging. Since I was speechless, support came from an unexpected quarter. Meri said, in her clear, precise way, "Lucy is in the business of selling wool, not spells. She is a very good mistress, fair and kind."

I was trying to curb her habit of calling me her mistress, but at least she'd stopped standing up and bowing whenever I walked in the room. Progress happened in small steps.

"Of course, she is, dear. But we'd like to suggest Violet come and work with you, as well, just to keep an eye on things."

My eyes nearly bugged out of my head. My cousin Violet, who'd pretty much challenged me to a witch's duel over our family grimoire, was not someone I trusted completely. Having her working for me seemed like a dodgy proposition.

"Violet's got excellent qualifications. She's a good knitter and has plenty of retail experience."

Violet hadn't said a word, so I turned to her. "Do you want to come and work for me?"

She shrugged, looking like she didn't much care either way. "I could use the extra money. Besides, now that you've got this market stall, it looks like you're going to have to leave Meri alone in the shop quite a bit. I already know she's a witch, and I can help teach her about things." She looked at me full on. "I'll do my best. I promise."

I really could use the extra help. And it would be nice not to worry about Meri every time I stepped out of the door. However, I didn't want them to think I was a pushover. I did my best to look steely and tough. "Very well. But only for the busy holiday period. After that, we'll see."

"A wise decision," Margaret Twig said. I didn't like the slight tone of menace in her voice. I couldn't help but recall the woman had tried to steal my beloved familiar. What would she have done if I'd refused to employ Violet? I wouldn't have put it past her to make my shop invisible. I really needed to work harder at controlling my magic, just so I could counter her spells.

"I'll be there tomorrow at nine," Violet said.

"Come at eight-thirty, so I can train you." I didn't really need her that early, but I had to remind all of us who was the boss.

Then the three of them turned and headed for a booth selling rocks and crystals.

Rafe glanced between me and Meri. I held up my hand. "Not one word."

He said, "I'm all but speechless." Then, "Have you had a chance to tour the market, yet?"

"I haven't."

"I would like to very much," Meri said.

I nodded. It was hard not to be drawn in, with all the lights, crowds of people walking up and down, the smell of German bratwurst in the air. So long as I dodged the three twisted sisters, it would be fun. He held out an arm to each of us and said, "I'll buy you both a Gluhwein."

I laughed. "Good thing our work day is over." But it was chilly and the hot, spiced wine sounded very good. He got us both a glass. After sniffing it suspiciously, Meri tasted it and decided it was very good. We wandered among the booths looking at pottery, hand-carved wooden toys, candles, quilted cushions, tiny felt animals. Then there was the food! Artisanal cheeses, honeys and jams, the warm, yeasty smell of bread, and chocolate.

When we'd circled the market and returned to Timeless Treasures, I followed instinct and walked across the street to the soap booth, Bubbles. The redhead was organizing her shelves, as she currently had no customers. I said, "Hi, it's Gemma, isn't it? I remember you from the orientation."

She glanced over and seemed pleased that I remembered her. "That's right. I can't remember your name, though, sorry."

"I'm Lucy. And this is Rafe and Meri. I'm helping with Timeless Treasures."

"You're busy. People are going crazy for those long stockings."

"You've been doing well, too. Who doesn't love handmade soaps?"

She laughed. "Yeah, I'm happy. If I was as busy as you I'd go crazy. It's only me, you see. A friend was supposed to help me but she got sick at the last minute and couldn't come." She shrugged. "So, it's just me."

That sucked. "Well, if I'm around and you need a break to go to the loo or grab a sandwich, or something, just let me know. I could fill in for you for a few minutes."

She looked truly grateful. "Thanks. Appreciate it."

Rafe asked, "Are you from Oxford?"

"No. Crawley, actually. In Sussex. But I've heard this is a good market. Always wanted to come."

He nodded. "Well, good luck."

He walked us home deep in thought. "What's on your mind?" I finally asked.

He glanced over at me. "Nothing, really. I was thinking that there are a lot of fine markets closer to Crawley than this one, that's all."

"I'm sure Gemma had her reasons for choosing Oxford."

"Yes. I'm sure she did."

$\mathcal{I}$ was walking down Broad Street heading toward the Christmas market. It was Sunday and my shop was closed, so I was free to help in Timeless Treasures. It was nearly noon and I was passing Weston Library, which is a newer complex, part of the Bodleian, but across the street from the grand, old library. Apart from the usual groups of students with their heavy book bags, shoppers, and tourists, I noted a line-up of people waiting in front of the double glass doors. I stopped to see what the attraction was and noticed a brand-new exhibition that had just opened. A large sign read: The Chronicles of Pangnirtung: Ancient Myth and Modern Legend. A Dominic Sanderson retrospective.

I'd have stepped around the end of the line, dodged the student walking his bike along the sidewalk, and kept going, but someone called my name. "Lucy?"

I turned to see Detective Inspector Ian Chisholm standing near the back of the line. He wore a navy blue coat done up against the cold and round his neck was a handknit scarf. Now that I owned a knitting shop, I noticed these things. I recognized the wool, and could take an educated guess at the dye lot. I suspected his aunt had knitted that scarf for him.

He was carrying a Bodleian Library shopping bag imprinted with the book cover of the first book in the Pangnirtung series. A painting of snow-capped mountains and in the foreground a small group of Katookuk, mythical creatures nearly as famous as Hobbits.

"I didn't peg you as a fantasy reader," I said, walking up to him.

He smiled his rather charming smile and the edges of his green eyes tilted upward. "It was these books that turned me into a reader. I loved them. I only wish Professor Sanderson had written more. This is the fortieth anniversary since they first came out, so they've published an anniversary edition, with a new introduction by the author, so that's something. I'm lining up now to get them signed."

Even though I wasn't a fantasy reader, I knew about the books. They'd been a massive, world-wide hit, spawned movies and merchandise. "Professor Sanderson still teaches at Oxford, doesn't he?"

"Yes. At Cardinal College, in fact, just down the road from your shop."

"I have to confess I never read the books. I saw the first movie, though. "

He made a *tsk* sound. "You know the movies aren't nearly as good as the books."

I shrugged. "Give me a good romance or mystery any day. I always struggle with fantasy."

"You don't believe that mythical creatures could have existed in lands long ago and far away?" His tone was teasing, but he didn't know that I lived with mythical creatures every day. They weren't long-ago or far away. They lived beneath my shop and knit sweaters. I supposed, being a witch, I was a bit of a mythical creature myself. "I prefer novels set in the real world."

The temperature must have been near freezing, as our breath made vapor trails as we spoke. "I suppose I see enough dark reality in my work. I read fiction to escape." The line edged forward and I took a step to keep talking to Ian. "What are you doing up this way? Obviously not going to see the Sanderson exhibit."

I laughed. "No. I'm peripherally involved in a craft booth selling knitted goods. It was set up by some of my customers. It's called Timeless Treasures."

"I'll have to stop by. Not that I need anymore knitted goods. Since my auntie's discovered your store, she keeps me well-stocked."

And, since his auntie didn't find it easy to get to Oxford from the village where she lived, it was usually Ian who came in to pick up the supplies for her. I was always happy to see him. I definitely had a little crush on him, and there was a certain expression in his eyes when he looked at me that made me think he might have warm feelings for me, too. However, we never acted on those feelings. I didn't know what his reasons were, but mine were that I didn't want a sharp eyed police officer getting too close to my secrets.

Still, he was good company and he'd proven to be a good friend. I always felt safer when he was around.

A sort of a quiet buzz went through the line and we both turned. Coming out of the door was a man, so full of importance he must be something to do with the exhibit. He was on the short side, heavily built and had a round face and full lips. He looked like a man who enjoyed food and all the pleasures of life. He wore a gray woolen overcoat and the top buttons were undone so I could see a cheerful blue and yellow bow tie. He said, in a loud, reverberating voice, "Thank you all for coming out today. I'm Charles Beach, Dominic Sanderson's agent. Volunteers will be going down the line and collecting your names. Professor Sanderson regrets he won't have time to put any special messages in your book. Just the name you write down and his signature. And, please, no questions. Dominic only has limited time."

Ian shook his head, looking disappointed. "I was hoping for a bit more. Maybe a chance to tell him how much his books have meant to me. Sounds like an assembly line, though, doesn't it?"

I had to admit, it did. He stepped out of the line. "I'll walk with you down to the market instead."

"It's going to be a good market, this year," I said. Having been at the planning meeting I knew that they were expecting a record number of craftspeople.

He nodded. "I just hope everyone behaves."

"And buys lots of lovely handcrafted gifts."

He chuckled. "You're becoming quite the entrepreneur."

I hadn't thought about it, but I supposed I was. I cared about how well my shop did, and I'd grown to care about my suppliers, the people who crafted artisanal yarns, and my customers who put their time and energy into making beautiful garments. The shop earned enough for me to live and hire an assistant, but the margins were tight and I was quite happy scheming of ways to improve the bottom line. I'd gone to business college for two years and I was glad that I understood how to read a balance sheet and the basics of running a business.

We both moved to the left to give a woman pushing a stroller toward us more room and then Ian put an arm around me and pulled me closer to him as a cyclist dodging a van nearly crashed into me. He dropped his arm immediately but I liked the way his cop's eyes were always looking ahead, watching out for trouble.

The crowds grew thicker the closer we got to the market. I could hear a school choir singing holiday favorites, see the twinkly lights in the brightly decorated booths, and shoppers happily crowding around them for that unique stocking present.

And speaking of stockings as we grew closer to Timeless Treasures I could see a woman lining up to pay, with four of the handmade stockings hanging over her arm. Behind her another woman, presumably her friend since they were chatting together, had two draped over her arm. I was going to have to put all the knitting vampires onto turning out stockings if we were going to keep up with the demand.

It was less busy across the street at Bubbles and so I led Ian over there. I may have had an ulterior motive in trying to keep him as far away from the vampires as I could. Gemma was using a big knife to cut a solid block of her handmade soap into smaller pieces. The soap was a pale purple and I could smell the lavender essential oil she'd mixed into it. There were little dots of lavender like purple freckles in the soap. I introduced the two of them, leaving out the fact that Ian was a cop, since he wasn't on duty. I explained that it was Gemma's first year at the market.

"Enjoying it so far?" Ian asked. It was an innocent enough question.

To my surprise, her face grew dark. "What's in the bag?" she asked.

Ian didn't get ruffled. He dealt with ruder people than her every day. He held the bag up. "They put out a new illustrated edition, for the fortieth anniversary. I bought it for myself as an early Christmas gift."

Gemma went back to cutting soap, using so much force the bars of soap bounced on her board. Ian and I exchanged a puzzled glance and he said, "Not a fan of fantasy?"

She glanced up and back at her soap. "Not a fan of the author."

Ian took a step back, as though he didn't want his precious books too close to that cleaver. "Well, I'll let you get on with it. I hope you have a successful market."

She nodded and muttered what could have been thank you and we moved away. When we were out of hearing, I said, "What was that about?"

He shrugged. "The author, Dominic Sanderson, is a notoriously tough professor. Perhaps he gave her a bad mark."

I glanced back at Gemma. Her lips were pressed in a tight line. She began wrapping the newly chopped bars of soap with strips of hand-made paper. I could just glimpse the silver from the pen she'd used to write the names of the soap on the paper labels. "Perhaps."

"If you'd told her I was a police officer, I might've thought she had reason to dislike my sort."

"You mean, she might have been in trouble with the law?"

He shrugged. "It's been known to happen."

We'd come to the edge of Broad Street and St. Giles and we both hesitated. He said, "I don't suppose you—"

"Lucy! Thank goodness. I thought that was you." It was Clara, who'd taken the first shift in the booth, with the help of Alfred. "Excuse me for interrupting, but we're going to run out of stockings. People have been telling their friends and they're coming, specially to buy them. Also, can you take some of the cash to the bank? I don't like having so much in the booth."

"Of course," I turned to Ian. "I'm sorry, you were saying?"

He shook his head, looking rueful. "Doesn't matter. You're obviously busy. Hope you have a successful day."

I watched as he strode away, book bag swinging from his hand. I wondered very much how that sentence would have ended?

$\mathscr{I}$ collected the sizable amount of cash, as discreetly as possible, and then headed back towards Cardinal Woolsey's with a list of items I was to bring back, mainly stockings.

I hadn't walked far when I felt a cool shiver run down my neck. Even though it was December, and cold, this was a particular kind of chill that meant Rafe was in the vicinity. Sure enough, he materialized by my side, as tall and brooding as ever.

"Is this a social call?" I asked him as he strode beside me, silent.

"I'm keeping an eye on you with all that money. I don't want you to be robbed."

I glanced up at him from under my lashes. "Worried about my safety?"

He glanced down at me. "Protecting the profits from our first Christmas market."

I burst out laughing. I couldn't help it. His sense of humor was so dry I was sometimes tempted to dust it. "Timeless

Treasures is doing remarkably well."

He nodded. "If this keeps up, we'll turn a nice profit." Rafe had never taken business college that I knew of, but in his six centuries on earth he'd obviously run quite a few businesses and amassed several fortunes. Yet, he was as pleased as I was to see the tiny holiday stall making money.

"Have you decided what charity you're going to support?"

He shook his head. "Not yet. I imagine we'll end up taking a vote when the market is over. Those of us who walk the streets at night see the homeless. Perhaps we can do something for them. Naturally, I always believe in supporting the work of the Bodleian." Rafe was an antiquarian and rare book expert, and often did work for the Bodleian Library. "The money won't go to waste."

He walked with me to the bank, where I deposited the cash into the night safe drop box, and then to Harrington Street. Above the closed shop, my flat was packed with vampires knitting with astonishing speed. I gathered up two dozen of the newest Christmas stockings, a few more children's sweaters and children's hats and woolen mittens. I said to Gran, "Clara says to put all your efforts into the stockings. They're outselling everything else four to one."

Gran was delighted and clapped her hands, though I imagined everyone in the room had heard me. She said, "Right, everybody? Finish whatever you're working on now, and then we're all to work on Christmas stockings."

Hester, the eternal teenager, rolled her black lined eyes heavenward, groaned, and slouched back on the couch. "I'm sick of knitting stockings. Why can't I make something else?"

Sylvia snapped at her. "This is the season of gift giving and goodwill. Nobody wants your depressing black shrouds."

Hester frowned but Sylvia wasn't far off. The teenager's latest obsession had been to knit endlessly long black wraps that were anything but cheerful.

"Fine," she said with a scowl. "I'll knit something nauseatingly cheerful with little yellow duckies and bunny rabbits all over it."

Gran looked at her with pity. "That's for Easter, Hester dear. This time of year we want reindeer and snowmen, Christmas baubles and trees laden with snow."

"I feel nauseous." She got off the couch and dragged herself to the table where all the wools and patterns and notions were stored. She helped herself to red and green wool and was soon busily handcrafting one of the very popular Christmas stockings.

Gran watched Hester with exasperated affection, which was pretty much how most of us regarded Hester most of the time. She said, "Hester was the clever one who created the extra long stockings. And look at how popular they've become."

Hester glared at her. "I was bored and forgot to cast off, that's all. They were never meant to be this long." But I could tell she was pleased to be acknowledged for her design, however it had come about.

"What do you think of this one, Lucy?" Dr. Christopher Weaver asked. He was meticulous in all his projects, and, when I looked at the stocking he was working on, I had a sneaking suspicion he'd only brought it to my attention so that I could praise him. And it was, indeed, the most beautiful piece. He'd created an old-fashioned Christmas tree, with candles instead of electric bulbs, and all the baubles and the candles were fashioned out of gold, silver, and jewel-colored threads. I said, "We're going to have to charge more for that one. It's exquisite."

Hester immediately threw her needles down and made a rude noise. "What's mine then, something for the bargain bin?"

I couldn't believe I'd been so tactless. I opened my mouth to say how valuable every contribution was, when Gran caught my eye and shook her head slightly. She said, "I think, Hester dear, that we have to price our stockings according to the work that's gone into them, the attention to detail, and the final product. That doesn't make yours dull, or pedestrian, just a little more basic."

"Basic?" shrieked Hester. "I'll show you basic." And then she marched over to the table where we kept all the supplies and chose some tiny sparkling crystals and lengths of jewel-colored thread.

I looked Gran who nodded knowingly and then winked at me. Oh, she was good.

Hester now sat down and took her stocking seriously, determined to make hers more beautiful than anything Christopher Weaver could create. In fact, a healthy sense of competition entered the room and work that had perhaps begun to grow tedious was now suddenly infused with creative spirit and one upmanship.

When I had collected, not only twenty-four stockings that were all wonderful, and brightly colored, but also the five deluxe stockings that Christopher Weaver had made, as well as the other items that Clara had specified, I headed back toward the market. The day was cold and cloudy, but no one seemed to mind. The Sunday afternoon crowd was at its thickest. I'd planned to help out at Timeless Treasures, but, once we'd displayed the new stock, Clara and Alfred clearly didn't need me. In such a small space I was only in the way. I thought I might wander around and perhaps get something to eat, when I noticed that Gemma had a crowd of people around her soap stall. It seemed she was struggling to keep up with them all.

She'd been rude and peculiar earlier, but it was her first market, and I hated to see anyone overwhelmed. I knew well what it was like to feel overburdened in a new retail enterprise. I hesitated only long enough to close my eyes and reach out to her with my mind. I immediately picked up her distress, so I slipped behind the table beside Gemma and asked, "Who's next in line, please?"

I hadn't asked permission and she cut her eyes to me. But Gemma didn't look annoyed by my interference; she looked desperately grateful. I was no expert on soap, but I could take money, make change, wrap packages, and wish people Happy Holidays. Any questions about ingredients, shelf life, whether this particular soap was good for dry skin, and so on I referred to Gemma. We worked surprisingly well together, manoeuvring comfortably around each other in the small space. It didn't take me long to pick up the basics. That one there was made with goat's milk, the Castile soap was pure olive oil and unscented, so very good for sensitive skin, this one here had oatmeal and was excellent for exfoliating. A cheerful older woman said, "I'd better take half a dozen assorted soaps, and four bottles of that lovely bath oil. Now I've bought these extra long stockings from across the way I need more gifts to stuff them with."

I said, making change, "Your family will be delighted."

"I think so, too. I can imagine these stockings in my family for years to come."

When things wound down, finally, Gemma let out a breath. "Phew." She shook her head. "I don't know what I would've done without you."

"You would've managed."

"Or lost my mind."

"Don't you have any help at all?" I didn't think she could manage the whole market all on her own.

She was tidying things up, adding stock to her displays. "I told you. I had a friend who was going to help me, but then her boyfriend got sick and she had to stay behind."

"Oh, that's too bad." In fact, she'd told me her friend was the one who got sick. Maybe there was no friend and she felt embarrassed not to be able to afford help.

"I'll manage on my own. I'll have to."

"Well, any time I'm around, I'm happy to help."

"Look, you really saved me. Let me buy you a drink when we're done."

I'd planned an early night—after an hour or so spent studying my grimoire—but I sensed that Gemma was lonely. If her friend had let her down, maybe she needed someone to talk to. Besides, I didn't have many friends my own age, I needed to put some effort into making some new ones. "Sure."

Once the market was closed and we'd shut and locked our chalets for the night, I led Gemma a little way down Cornmarket Street to The Crown, a pub whose main claim to fame was that Shakespeare made it his headquarters when he was travelling between Stratford and London. It also had a great atmosphere, lots of cozy corners to sit in, and good food.

We both sighed when we sat down and got the weight off our feet. Standing on hard pavement for hours was not the easiest activity on the body. I stretched my aching feet out in front of me.

"What can I get you?" Gemma said, standing up. "I'm going to have some of their hot, spiced wine."

At the end of a chilly evening, that sounded like a great idea, so I said I'd have the same.

She soon returned with the hot drinks and we clinked glasses and sipped. It was lovely, winey and spicy and the drink warmed me all the way to my aching toes.

We looked at each other and I could see us both searching for that first get-to-know-you question. Finally, she said, "So, where's home for you? You sound American."

I smiled at that. A few months ago, I would've struggled to answer that question. However, in the time I'd lived here, I had embraced Oxford, Cardinal Woolsey's, the nest of vampires living beneath me, and was beginning to accept the magic within me. I said, "Oxford is home. I was born in Boston, though. I mainly grew up there, but I spent most of my summers here, working at Cardinal Woolsey's Knitting Shop, with my grandmother. She passed away a few months ago and left me the shop. And now I live here and I run a knitting shop."

"I'm sorry about your grandmother. Were you close?"

I nodded. "We were." And that hadn't changed. At this very moment Gran was conducting two dozen knitting vampires, encouraging them to turn out their best work. She might be undead, but I adored her.

"How about you?" I asked. "Where are you from?"

"London. Well, the outskirts of London. Crawley. Mum

was a teacher. That's where she found a job, so that's where we moved when I was little." She sighed. "I lost her last year, to cancer."

"I'm so sorry for your loss."

"Thanks. It's hard because we were best friends." She didn't mention a father, so I didn't pry.

"I've never been to Crawley. But that's no surprise, there's a lot of England I haven't seen. It's hard to find the time to travel and run a shop."

She nodded. "Plus, Oxford is so pretty, living here must be like being on holiday, all the time."

We chatted until our glasses were empty and then faced that moment when we had to decide whether we were going to say goodbye, have another drink, or stay for something to eat. I was now warm, comfortable, and the thought of going home and trying to make my dinner in the midst of a knitting factory did not appeal. I was positive I'd be assigned a non-knitting menial task like rolling wool or something. I'd already done my bit, so I thought staying here seemed much more interesting. Besides, I liked Gemma. I wanted to get to know her. So, when she motioned to my empty glass and said, "Another?"

I said, "I tell you what. I'll let you buy me another drink and I'll buy us dinner."

She argued that she'd be taking advantage but I explained that I didn't feel like cooking and she'd be doing me a favor and, in the end, she agreed. I am particularly partial to shepherd's pie and so, it turned out, was she. We both had shepherd's pie and, instead of more mulled wine, each had a glass of red wine.

As we settled over food, we grew more relaxed with each

other. The fact that we'd already worked together for a few hours had broken the ice. I asked, "Do you make soap and personal beauty products as a full-time job?"

"Oh, no. I do it as a hobby. I'm taking my teacher training. I do this to help cover my bills while I'm at school."

"Were you able to find accommodation?" I knew that finding a place to stay in Oxford was notoriously expensive. If I hadn't already had Meri staying in my spare bedroom I might've invited Gemma to stay with me while the market was going on. She said, "I was able to get a deal on a hotel room in Botley. It's fine, and the bed's comfortable."

"Good." I remembered her strange reaction to Dominic Sanderson's fantasy trilogy and Ian's theory that she'd received a poor grade from the notoriously picky professor. "Did you go to one of the colleges here?"

She laughed and shook her head. "Even if I'd had the grades, I could never have afforded to come to school here. No, I had to be close enough so that I could live at home. Mum supported me while she could. My dad did his best, but he's got no money."

I was incurably nosy, and I couldn't seem to leave the subject alone. "You seemed pretty angry about Dominic Sanderson."

She pushed a bit of mashed potato around with her knife and I thought she wasn't going to answer. Finally, she said, "My dad and Dominic Sanderson were close friends here at Oxford. But Sanderson was a bad friend. He ruined my father's life."

I wasn't entirely sure I had heard her correctly. A university friend had ruined her father's entire life? She had to be thirty, so this life-ruining thing must've happened a long time ago. "Must have been quite something to have ruined his whole life."

"It's a long story." She chuckled, bitterly. "In fact, it's three long stories."

I might not be a literary genius, but I had to assume she was referring to Sanderson's fantasy trilogy. Especially, since she had acted so hostile to seeing the bag in Ian's hand. Nothing I'd seen before or since had led me to believe she was an angry person, but where Sanderson and that book were concerned, she was angry.

She shook her head. "I shouldn't have said anything. It's just so weird being here. I wonder if coming to Oxford was a mistake?" She seemed to be speaking to herself, so I sat there and listened. She glanced up at me and then back at her half-empty glass of wine. "Truth is, I needed to get away from a guy."

"Oh, no." I knew all about getting away from bad break ups. I'd come about four thousand miles to forget Todd the Toad. I waited, in case she wanted to say more, not wanting to pry, but we were a couple of single, straight women out in the pub, getting to know each other. Of course, we were going to talk about guys.

She pushed her copper hair over her shoulder with one impatient hand. A silver ring glinted from her finger. "His name's Darren. I met him in the pub when I was out with some friends. Seemed nice enough. Okay looking. He chatted me up and I gave him my number. He called and we went out a few times."

A couple walked by our table, arguing. She was telling him they'd be late if they didn't get going and he insisted they had time for another pint. He was a hefty bloke and he knocked our table as they went by. The table jerked so violently that both our wine glasses started to tumble. I muttered a spell under my breath, faster than I could reach the glass with my hand, and the glasses tilted straight again, table and wine stilled instantly. If I'd been thinking I wouldn't have done it, but magic was becoming second nature to me.

The grumpy guy was still arguing for his pint and hadn't noticed the almost-disaster, but I was terrified Gemma would look at me in fear and drag me straight to a witch trial. She only stared, then giggled. "That was weird."

I forced a laugh, too. "Yeah. I totally thought they were going to spill."

"Shakespeare must be looking out for us."

Absolutely, blame it on Shakespeare!

"So," I prompted, "Darren?"

"Yes." She sighed. "Darren. Not one of my better decisions. We dated a few times and he started getting possessive, talking about the future in unnerving ways, like how many children we were going to have. He was getting his gas-fitter's license and working out where I could get a teaching job and he could get hired on with a good company. He had it all planned out. When we'd buy a house and have our first child."

"Seriously? After only a few dates? I was with my last boyfriend for two years and when I talked about moving to the next stage of our relationship, he went and slept with somebody else." We all had our issues.

"I wish Darren would. I told him to slow down, I wasn't ready, and then he started acting really strange. Showing up outside my house. I'd get off school and he'd be there, on his motorbike, waiting for me."

It sounded horrendous. I felt creeped out just hearing about this guy. "What did you do?"

She leaned forward and her hair caught the light, copper, brass, and hints of gold. "I broke up with him, of course." She blew out a breath. "That's when he threatened to kill himself."

"Oh, no."

"Yeah. I'm so stupid, I believed him. I tried to get him help. But all he wanted was my attention."

"I'm so sorry."

She nodded. "It's one of the reasons I came here. I'm hoping if I'm out of town, he'll move on or forget about me."

"Seriously? That's why you came to Oxford?"

"Well, I also wanted to come and see it. Dad was a student here and—I think this is where he was happiest." She looked uncomfortable suddenly. "You're a good listener. I'm talking too much."

"No. This is what women do. We support each other." I hesitated to give advice, but she'd been honest enough to tell me her problems, I couldn't sit here and not give her some candid feedback. "Have you talked to the police?"

She dropped her gaze to the table top. "No. What would I say? Darren hasn't done anything. He never threatened me, only himself." She glanced at her cell phone. "It's getting late. I should get back."

"Yes, so should I."

We both stood and then she turned to me. "Thank you so much, again, for helping me out today."

"Hey, when I was first struggling to find my way around Cardinal Woolsey's I had some help, too. I don't know what I would've done without it. I'm just paying it forward."

She nodded. "And one day I'll do the same."

"Deal."

We didn't make a big deal of goodbyes, since we'd see each other tomorrow. She headed off to get a bus that would take her to her hotel, and I walked home. The quickest way home was going straight down Cornmarket, but I didn't always feel like taking the most obvious path. I was still finding my way around this fascinating city and so I took the slightly longer way round, down Queen Street and New Inn Hall Street which crosses the top end of Harrington Street.

The rest had done my feet good, but I was glad I didn't have too long a walk ahead of me. I was accompanied by the clicking sound of my boots on pavement and my thoughts, which centred on my new acquaintance, Gemma.

I felt that she was troubled by more than what she'd told me, and wondered if I'd ever have enough of her confidence that she would tell me why she was really here.

There was a time, not so very long ago, when I might have pressed, convinced that it was good to share troubles. However, since I had lived in Oxford, I'd come to understand that some secrets can't be shared. So, I hadn't pried.

I stopped walking. I didn't turn around, or even search the shadows, I simply stopped walking and said aloud, "I know you're there."

CHAPTER 5

a soft chuckle greeted my words and Rafe appeared at my side. "You always accuse me of appearing like a puff of smoke. I can't believe you heard me over the infernal noise you're making with those boots."

I hid my smile. He was irked that I had sensed his presence. "I didn't hear you. I felt you. It's like a cool tingle on the back of my neck."

He looked at me intensely. Now I realized I only got that tingle with him, not the other vampires, and if he asked, I'd have to tell him that. And then he would wonder why he affected me that way. Unless he already knew. "It must be my witchy sense," I said.

He was still looking at me in that intense, broody way he had. "No doubt."

"So, are you just out for a stroll? Or are you following me?" In truth, I hadn't felt him when I was in the pub, only since I'd left.

He walked at my side for a couple more steps and then said, "I don't have to follow you. I sense you, too."

"Really? You get a tingle on the back of your neck?"

Once more that silence that went on a beat too long. Finally, he said, "I can smell you."

Oh, how I wished I had never started this conversation. I knew he meant me no harm, but when a vampire said, "I can smell you," it did not fill me with warm and fuzzy feelings. The words cold-blooded killer flitted across my mind before I could shake them away.

He said, "We both have senses we can't control. But we can keep our impulses in check."

I didn't look at him. I just nodded. I searched for something to say that would move away from this intensely awkward conversation but he got there first. "How was your evening?"

"It was good. Gemma seems really nice. But she has a sadness about her." We walked on. "You've been in Oxford a long time, haven't you?"

"Probably too long. I'm going to have to move on, soon."

"Oh, no." The words were out before I could stop them. I didn't want him to leave Oxford. I couldn't imagine not having Rafe in my life.

"Part of the curse of being a nightwalker and mingling with mortals is that we don't age. I'm beginning to hear the joke about being Dorian Gray. He's the Oscar Wilde character who sold his soul to the devil in order to retain his youthful looks."

"I know who Dorian Gray is," I said, scornfully. Sure, he knew a lot more than I did, but I wasn't completely lacking in literary knowledge. Then I thought about the idea of selling one's soul to stay forever young. "I guess, in a way, you did."

"You mistake," he said with bitterness. "I didn't choose this existence, it was forced upon me."

"Of course it was," I said quietly." I'm sorry."

He shrugged. "One becomes accustomed."

He couldn't change his fate, but he could choose where he lived. "You won't leave very soon, will you?"

His gaze held mine. He shook his head. "No. I won't be leaving anytime soon."

I could breathe a little easier knowing he'd be staying. One day, I'd have to say good-bye to Rafe, but I was very glad it wasn't going to be today. "Gemma seems very angry with Dominic Sanderson."

"The author?"

"Yes. She said he ruined her father's life. They used to be students together, here in Oxford. I know it was a long time ago, and a lot of students go through here, but I just wondered if, by any chance, you might have heard rumors?"

"Of course. That's why she seemed so familiar to me." He sounded quite pleased. "It's been driving me mad. I knew I'd never met her personally, at least I thought I hadn't, but there was a familiarity about her." He walked on in silence for a full minute and I left him to his reverie, knowing he would share his thoughts when he was ready. Finally, he said, "Yes, it's all coming back to me now. What's her surname?"

I'd seen her name on the list of all the booth owners, but I hadn't memorized all the names. "I think it's Gemma Hitchins? Hodkins? Something like that."

He snapped his fingers, the unexpected crack of sound making me jump. "Not Hodgkins, Hodgins. Yes. Martin Hodgins must be her father. She has a similar look." We walked on. "There was an unpleasant scandal at the time.

Forty years ago or more, I suppose, Dominic Sanderson and Martin Hodgins were students together and friends. Inseparable, really. Both studied English literature as I recall, at Cardinal College. Both had very promising futures. They were extremely bright, studious, and stayed out of trouble. Great things were predicted for both of them."

"Well, certainly Dominic Sanderson has enjoyed an illustrious career."

"Oh yes. Brilliant. Not only is he a distinguished professor but those books, well, I don't need to tell you. It's not every fantasy novel writer who is honored by a retrospective of their work at the Bodleian." I stifled a smile. I got the feeling that he wasn't entirely approving of living fantasy authors getting retrospectives at the Bodleian.

"But what happened to the other student? His friend and, presumably, Gemma's dad?"

He shook his head. "It was very sad. Or foolish. Or both. Martin Hodgins was in his last year. He'd nearly made it to the end when he submitted a paper that contained large passages that were not his own work. Of course, in those days, there were no computer programs that scanned every student's essay and detected similarities to published work. He might've got away with the plagiarism if the professor doing the marking hadn't recognized the source material. Naturally, he was caught. And sent down. He never received his degree. He was rather in disgrace."

I felt there was more to the story so I waited. Sure enough, Rafe continued, "But, it didn't end there. A year later, Dominic Sanderson sold his fantasy trilogy. He was in the right place, at the right time, with the right agent. Still, it was an extremely lucrative deal for a first time author, especially one so young, and he got quite a bit of publicity, as you can imagine."

"He sold three completed novels a year after he graduated?" I'd only managed two years of business college, but I couldn't imagine turning around and writing three massive fantasy novels right afterward. Or even during my studies.

"Oh yes, he was in his early twenties. I think that contributed to his celebrity status."

I was still thinking about the timing. "But, he must have written them while he was at Oxford. He couldn't possibly have written the Chronicles of Pangnirtung in only a few months."

"You're right. He'd written most of them while a student. Well, the next thing that happened was that Martin Hodgins claimed the fantasy trilogy had been his idea all along. It was dreadfully embarrassing. I believe Hodgins even hired a lawyer and tried to sue. But, of course, Dominic Sanderson had the original manuscripts and his publisher and agent stood by him and put their considerable resources into fighting the claim. Meanwhile, Martin Hodgins had already been discredited as a plagiarist." He shook his head. "No one likes to see a promising young man end like that."

"What happened to him? Martin Hodgins?" He was interesting to me because he was Gemma's dad.

"I don't know. He disappeared."

"That must be what Gemma meant when she said that Dominic Sanderson had ruined her father's life."

"I rather think her father ruined his own life."

"She was brought up by her mother, I got the feeling she was pretty much a single parent. She said her father did his best but he had no money. I guess he never recovered from the scandal." Poor Gemma. I'd grown up with two professor parents and, while life with a couple of geniuses was far from perfect, I'd always been proud of them and their accomplishments. What must it be like to grow up with someone who'd started out so promising and ended so badly?

As THE FOLLOWING WEEK PROGRESSED, I began to think that every fireplace mantelpiece in all of Oxfordshire would feature extra long hand-knitted stockings this year. If we hadn't had more than twenty vampires with extraordinary speed and skill knitting all night long, we never could've kept up with the demand. As it was, I made two trips to the bank most days and Meri or I kept delivering an incredible assortment of stockings.

I got into the habit of returning to help close up and taking the last deposit, in its special pouch, to the bank's night safe drop box. I also popped by a couple of times a day to check stock or even help with the selling. I hated to admit it, but hiring Violet had been a great idea. She had lots of retail experience and she could knit, plus, my grandmother was just upstairs if she had any questions. Meri might not be the hippest girl on the planet, but she was an incredibly hard worker and had a sweetness about her that just drew people. I thought sometimes that they bought more than they intended to make her happy. Of course, she had no idea of the effect she had on people, which was part of her selling superpower.

Violet and Meri got on well, too. I think because Meri considered me as her new mistress, akin to the pharaoh's demanding wife in her last gig, she was never quite as relaxed around me. But Violet was another witch working in the shop, so she could let her guard down and ask her questions that she hesitated to ask me.

It was fun working outside at the Christmas market. Sure, it was much harder on the feet and legs to be standing all day on pavement, and I had to bundle up warm because of the chill in the air, but I was not short of hand-knitted sweaters, coats, gloves, and hats, so I managed to stay toasty warm.

It was Wednesday afternoon and the day was heavy with unshed rain. I headed to Timeless Treasures with twenty-five stockings so freshly knitted I swear they were warm. I glanced up at the brooding, dark clouds, wondering when the first drops would fall. I had my rain jacket in my bag just in case.

The market was bustling in spite of the threatened rain. I could smell gingerbread, and chocolate, and as I grew closer I could smell the delicate fragrances—all natural, she assured me–emanating from Bubbles, Gemma's soap store.

There was a good crowd gathered around Timeless Treasures and I immediately stepped up to help. A woman I recognized as one of Cardinal Woolsey's customers came up wearing a sweater she'd knitted herself from wool and pattern that I'd sold her. "Well, hello, Lucy. Isn't this fun?" She handed me five of the long stockings. "I could knit these myself, but I can't keep up with my knitting projects as it is."

I laughed and told her I completely understood the appeal of purchasing things that were already finished. When I'd taken her money and given her change, she gathered up her stockings. "I'll just pop them in here." Her bag was from the Sanderson retrospective. Half the people wandering around the market seemed to have come from the exhibit.

Clara surreptitiously passed me a fat envelope of cash to deposit. Her eyes were sparkling. "We're doing so well," she said. "I had no idea running a market stall could be so entertaining. You see such an interesting cross-section of people."

I loved their enthusiasm. I'd kept an eagle eye on the vampires the first couple of days, in case they should get hungry, but someone, no doubt Dr. Weaver, was making sure that they were fed regularly, so they were never tempted by the smorgasbord of humanity walking up and down in front of them.

There were quite a few shoppers milling around Bubbles. I glanced at Gemma, ready to give her a wave by way of greeting and stopped, with my hand half raised. Gemma looked as though she were on the verge of tears. Her eyes were red-rimmed and over bright, and her smile looked forced.

I didn't know what to do. She was busy, but not overwhelmed with customers. Had someone been rude to her? I hovered in the background and she glanced up, as though she felt me there. She motioned me forward with one hand and then went back to serving her current customer.

I walked into her chalet and stood beside her. She leaned closer to me. "Can you take over for a few minutes? I've got to get out of here."

I'd been right, she was close to tears. I could hear the tremble in her voice. Naturally, I told her to take as much time as she needed. I was in no hurry. She nodded gratefully, finished up with her customer, and then, excusing herself, left the booth.

I put on a professional smile. "Yes, how can I help you?" I asked the next person in line. She was a young mother pushing a sleeping baby in a pram and she asked which soaps were the most gentle. Fortunately, I'd spent enough hours in the stall already that I could answer most of her questions. Gemma had soap and shampoo specifically for babies, which the woman happily purchased, along with some soaps as gifts for her co-workers.

I got the feeling she needed some pampering, herself, so I said, "You have to smell these bath salts. They've got lavender in them and special salts and minerals. After a long day at work, when you've finally got the baby to sleep, you should treat yourself to a nice bath with these." I took the stopper out of the sample bottle and offered it to her. After an appreciative sniff she agreed and bought herself several packages.

As I was wrapping her purchase, I watched Gemma. She hadn't gone far and was acting very strangely. She seemed to be searching for someone. She walked up and down, her eyes constantly searching the crowd. She didn't look hopeful of seeing an old friend. I felt her distress so keenly my chest tightened. My witch powers did not come without a price.

An older man came up. He was holding one of the Sanderson retrospective bags and it was so bulging I suspected he'd really gone to town in the gift shop. I was happy Gemma wasn't around to see it. He asked if I could recommend something for his wife, who loved roses. I shifted my gaze from Gemma and smiled at him. "I have the perfect gift." I offered him another sample bottle to sniff. "These bath salts contain actual rose petals as well as essence of roses, neroli, and a complex blend of other essential oils. I think it smells like a rose garden on a sunny afternoon." If Gemma had been there she would've itemized every one of those oils and scents, but I couldn't remember them all. I was thinking on my feet here.

He seemed quite pleased with my answer and happily bought his wife the bath salts. I suggested the matching soap, which was a lovely pale pink color. I was able to tell him the color was achieved, not with artificial dye, but with French pink clay, that was also very good for the complexion. He also bought the body cream and a dry skin ointment marketed for men.

He looked about him as though not quite sure what else he might purchase. I leaned forward. "If you're looking for something to put those in, may I recommend the extra long stockings over at Timeless Treasures? They've been very popular this year. People seem to love them." I couldn't think of a reason why Gemma and I shouldn't promote each other's goods.

He raised his brows and looked over at the knitting stall. "What a good idea. Why, I haven't had a Christmas stocking since I was a boy."

"You and your wife should start a new tradition. Buy two stockings and you can fill them with fun little gifts for each other."

He looked as delighted as he probably had when he'd opened his stocking when he was that little boy. "That's a wonderful idea. Thank you, my dear."

It was nearly an hour before Gemma returned. I'd seen her a few more times in my peripheral vision, wandering around the market, obviously searching for someone. I had no idea what was going on and, anyway, I was kept busy packing soaps and enticing browsers closer so I could turn them into purchasers.

I liked the challenge of helping a shopper find the right gift. Plus, I thought that Gemma needed all the profits she could earn from her stint at the market.

She returned at last, looking almost more upset than she had before she left. As soon as there was a lull I asked, "Is everything all right?" It was a leading question, of course, since it was very clear that everything was not all right with my new friend Gemma.

She shook her head, sharply. Glanced up and down out of narrowed eyes and said, "Darren, my ex-boyfriend is here."

No wonder she was upset. "Are you sure?"

"He texted me and said he had to see me. I told him not to come. I don't want to see him. I broke up with him. We're done." She vibrated with negative energy. "I don't even know how he found out I was in Oxford." Her voice rose.

"He probably did an Internet search. If he used your name and the name of your stall, you wouldn't be that difficult to find." Sometimes, the oh-so-connected world wasn't our friend.

She rubbed her arms as though she were cold. "He's acting like a stalker. It's horrible. I feel violated."

"I don't blame you." I couldn't imagine what I'd do if Todd a.k.a. The Toad suddenly decided to fly to England and try to win me back. Not that I was in any danger of that happening, since the only time he'd contacted me since we'd broken up was to ask if I had an old hoodie of his. It wasn't very flattering to my ego, but it was better than being stalked.

I asked, "What can I do?"

She shook her head, looking helpless. "I don't know. I

searched all around but now I can't find him. He didn't even come right up to the booth. He sort of hovered in the background, making sure I knew he was here, and then he disappeared."

"Maybe he left?" I said it more to comfort than because I thought her stalker had given up so easily.

"I wish. I can't stand knowing he's here, skulking around, watching me. If he'd come up and talk to me, I could tell him to go away. But having him hover around is doing my head in."

I didn't know if her ex was dangerous, but I didn't want to take chances. She'd be safe enough at the market with so many people about, but I didn't like the idea of her going to her hotel alone. I said, "Why don't you come home with me and stay the night?" Even as the words left my mouth I realized that was a terrible idea. Poor Gemma had enough problems right now, she did not need to walk into a nest of knitting vampires. Even as I tried to think how I might take back my spontaneous invitation, she was already shaking her head.

"I can't. I really appreciate it, but I've got a lot of product that I need to cut and wrap. I'll be busy all evening. But thanks."

We'd exchanged mobile numbers earlier, so I said, "Make sure you call me when you get to the hotel. If that creep bothers you, I'll come over to your place. You're not alone."

She got that look again, as though she might cry. "I can't tell you how much this means to me. I hardly even know you and you're already a good friend."

The rain came late that afternoon and I hoped it

drenched Darren and drove him, wet and miserable, back to wherever he'd come from.

~

THURSDAYS THE MARKET stayed open until eight, so it was a long day for the vampire sellers. The rain had pounded the city overnight, and the streets were still damp but it was clear and cold.

After dropping off yet another lot of stockings and a few more sweaters and scarves, I headed over to Bubbles. Gemma seemed calm enough and as soon as she'd finished with her latest customer, I asked, "Did you hear from him anymore?"

She rolled her eyes and pulled out her mobile. "I shouldn't have texted, I was just so furious." She showed me her text which read: *Please leave me alone.*

He'd replied almost immediately: *Just let me see you so I can explain. I love you. We're meant to be together.*

She rubbed the heel of her hand against her temple as though she was fighting a headache. "I didn't reply after that. I was a fool to contact him, you don't have to tell me."

"Hey, you have all my sympathy. Do you think he's gone?"

"I haven't seen him, so maybe?" She didn't look convinced.

I headed back over to Timeless Treasures and as I did, I glimpsed a man who stood out because he was doing exactly that. Standing. Not shopping, ambling from one stall to another, chatting or visiting. He stood, stock still, and he was watching Gemma. I glanced her way but she was busy with another customer and didn't see him.

My returning spell had been slightly disastrous when I'd

tried to send Margaret's hat home, but the circumstances had been peculiar. It had been Samhain and I must have harnessed the collective power of the assembled coven, plus the magic of the ancient stones themselves. I was certain that if I cast the spell again, focusing only on Darren, I could send him back to whatever hole he'd crawled from.

I hesitated, never having tried the spell on a living thing before. No, I decided. I could do it. I turned, ready to return Darren like a piece of rejected mail, only to find he'd already disappeared. Since I'd had nothing to do with his vanishing, I suspected he'd snuck away again.

I didn't think vampires could get tired, but at the end of the evening, both Clara and Mabel were complaining that their legs ached. They did look worn out. Of course, for them, working all day was like me working all night. I wasn't sure they were able to switch over their schedules and sleep at night. "You go on now," I said. "I'll finish closing up."

They didn't argue with me, simply nodded, gratefully, and headed home. After the market closed, it was like a circus breaking down. We pulled in all the displays and products and closed everything up in its cozy little shed for the night. The chalets each had a heavy padlock, but still, I wouldn't have wanted to leave anything too valuable inside. When I was finished with my stall, I went over and helped Gemma close up. Her face was flushed with excitement.

"Guess what? I made five hundred pounds profit today. Doing this market was really a good idea. It will help me make a dent in my student loans."

"That's great," I said. I was genuinely pleased for her. She seemed like someone who worked very hard and didn't always catch the breaks. She put her cash in a vinyl zip up bag, the kind they give away free with cosmetics bonuses. I said I'd walk up with her to the bank but she wanted to finish tidying up and so I went on alone.

I got to the bank and reached into my handbag for the envelope of cash from Timeless Treasures. It wasn't there. My heart lurched in a terrible moment of panic. Had I passed someone on the street who'd slipped his or her hand into my bag and taken the money without me noticing? I didn't remember brushing against anyone. And what was the point of being a witch if I could be pick-pocketed so easily?

Had I dropped the cash somewhere? I beat back the panicky feeling that I'd lost a great deal of money that didn't belong to me and then forced myself to think back and mentally retrace my steps. I'd dragged in the table that displayed goods for sale during the daytime. I remembered putting the envelope of cash on it while I put everything away. I'd locked up behind me, but, now I thought about it, I was almost certain I'd forgotten to pick up the cash when I left.

I leaned against the cold stone wall beside the bank's night safe drop box and groaned.

I did not want to retrace my steps. It was cold and dark and my feet were tired. But, I knew I'd never sleep for worrying if I didn't retrieve that money and deposit it. The cash was destined for charity, after all.

I stomped back toward the market, beating myself up mentally the whole time. How could I have been so stupid? I walked quickly, my breath making white puffs in the night air, and the heels of my boots echoing on the pavement of the deserted streets.

As I grew closer, the market, which was so cheerful and

inviting when filled with shoppers and glowing with lights, seemed dark and sad and deserted. I shivered, and then chided myself for being such a fool. Perhaps it was the wispy cloud trailing over the moon that made the scene look so eerie. The gothic arches, the spires and domes all appeared like ghosts from the past, looming in shadow, watching. I'd be glad to get the money safely deposited and head back to my warm flat. Gran had hinted that she might make a batch of gingerbread cookies today. Being surrounded by a group of vampires knitting feverishly, while crunching the world's best cookies, seemed like a really good idea right now.

CHAPTER 6

*a*s I grew closer to the huddle of dark chalets, I began to get that creeping feeling of being watched. Not the chill down the back of my neck that informed me Rafe was around, more like a nightmare feeling, when something dark and scary was chasing me and I couldn't run fast enough.

It was after nine and there didn't seem to be a soul about. I got out the keys and hurried my steps. When I got to the Timeless Treasures chalet, I glanced around nervously before unlocking the door. In the daytime, with the doors open and the lights on, with brightly colored goods spilling out, the market stall looked like a charming gingerbread-house-style chalet. But, essentially, when the doors were closed and it was locked up, it was a storage locker. I unlocked the padlock and eased the door open. Using the flashlight function on my mobile, I quickly discovered that I had, indeed, left the envelope of cash, already in its special pouch for deposit, sitting on the table.

Shaking my head in my own foolishness, I snatched up the envelope and tucked it into my bag.

I re-locked the door and turned around, breathing a quick sigh of relief, ready to walk home once again.

I'm not sure what made me look across at Gemma's chalet. Had I heard a noise? I turned in time to see a dark figure disappear between Gemma's stall and the one next to hers. I took a few steps forward, thinking that while I had any number of undead knitting friends looking out for me, and some genuine living friends, Gemma didn't know anyone in Oxford. If her chalet had been broken into, I should step up and be her friend. I knew how important the money was to her. I didn't want her to be robbed, not when she'd had such a good day. Since we had the bad boyfriend history in common, I knew how much she needed this Oxford experience to be a good one.

Her chalet looked quiet and undisturbed. I was tempted to turn away and walk home, but I had a nagging sense that all was not right. I wasn't always certain what was intuition, what was my witch powers, and what was irrational fear. Probably, I'd spooked myself and was seeing monsters under the bed that weren't there. However, on the off chance that my powers were tapping me on the shoulder, I figured I'd better take a closer look.

I'd just check that her lock was secure. That was all I'd do. It was neighborly. Friendly. Then I'd scamper home, make some hot chocolate to go with those cookies and sit in on the knitting circle for a while. The bank deposit would be safe with the vampires until tomorrow.

I squared my shoulders and walked briskly forward.

When I was close enough to see clearly, I realized that I didn't have to test her lock because the door was ajar.

The sense that all was not right deepened. I could feel blackness, like thick shadow, around the door. A splash of color emerged and I recognized the toe end of one of a Christmas stocking emerging through the crack in the open door. It looked as though someone had shut the door hastily behind them, but the foot end of the stocking had stopped the door from shutting all the way. I switched the flashlight back on and silver and gold threads caught the light.

Why would one of Christopher Weaver's Christmas stockings be in Gemma's chalet? I reached for the door and slowly opened it. Inside my woolen mitts my hands were shaking.

In movies and television shows when people—usually women—find dead bodies, they always scream their heads off. In my experience, that's not what happens. Or at least not with me. I saw Gemma, lying on her side, with her back to me, and one of our stockings, one of our beautiful handcrafted, meant-to-be-a-family-heirloom, stockings, was wrapped around her throat.

There was no blood or any signs of violence. Had the stocking been used to strangle her?

I didn't scream. I stood there, frozen, as the enormity of what I was looking at began to filter through my senses. Then, I dropped to my knees beside her. "Gemma?"

Sure, maybe it was stupid to call her name, but there was always the possibility that she'd somehow fallen asleep on the floor of her chalet. It wasn't very likely, but I was grasping at straws.

She didn't answer.

I pulled off one of my mittens, gently pushed her hair out

of her face and touched her cheek. It was cool, but not stone cold. She was more the temperature of Rafe or my Gran.

Don't be dead. Please, please don't be dead.

I picked up her wrist and felt for a pulse. My own was jumping so crazily that I wasn't sure, but I thought, maybe, I felt a very faint beat. This time, I spoke aloud. "Oh please, please, Gemma. Don't be dead."

I didn't scream, then, but I yelled. "Rafe!"

I knew he walked the streets at night, and I knew he was strangely connected with me. I believed that if I yelled for him he would come. And then I did what any other normal person would do and called 999.

It was awful seeing Gemma lying on the cold ground but I couldn't move her in case her neck was broken, or she was injured in some way that I could make worse by moving her. But the ground was so cold. I took off my coat and laid it over her. I also switched on the light in the chalet.

And then, because I didn't know what else to do, and I wanted to keep her alive, I began to rub her hands and to talk to her. "Gemma, it's Lucy. I'm here. I'm with you and I've called for an ambulance. You're safe now." *I really hoped that was true, for both our sakes.* "You've got to stay with me. Try and breathe. Just keep breathing."

I looked at that scarf wrapped so tightly around her neck and eased it away. My hands were shaking so badly I fumbled, but I managed to loosen her woolen noose.

Rafe arrived, and didn't say a word. He took in the scene at a glance and dropped to his knees beside me. "Is she dead?" He asked me softly, but in a matter-of-fact tone. If he'd tried to comfort me or express shock or sadness, I think I'd have burst into tears. His calm helped me to remain composed.

"I'm not sure. I think, maybe, she's still breathing, but I'm in such a state myself I can't tell."

Gently, he took her hand from mine and pressed his fingers against her wrist. He glanced up at me and he must've seen the anxiety in my eyes for he smiled, reassuringly. "There's definitely a pulse. It's not strong, but she's alive."

I was so happy I felt a stinging behind my eyelids. Then, he slipped off his coat and added it to mine on top of Gemma. I took her hand back and kept talking to her. I don't even know what I said, nonsense probably. I was talking for my own benefit as much as Gemma's.

Rafe said, "Did you call an ambulance?"

I nodded.

"Good." He turned his head, listening. His hearing was acute, much keener than mine. "The police are on their way, too."

He rose, and stepped out of the chalet. I could see him glancing up and down Broad Street. He turned back to me. "Did you see anyone? Hear anything?"

I recalled those creepy moments when I'd thought I'd heard something and then turned in time to see that figure running away. I recounted exactly what I'd sensed, and seen. "It might've just been some kind of intuition."

He nodded. "I'm glad you heeded your senses. You likely saved her life."

I hadn't thought of that. "You mean...?"

"Someone intended this young woman to be dead. And, because you were here, they didn't have time to finish the job."

I shivered all over. "I almost walked in on a murderer?"

He looked down at me. His eyes were cold and furious. "I believe so." Then he hesitated. "I felt that you were in trouble. I believe that I would always feel it, but even so, what the hell were you doing wandering around, alone, late at night?"

"Luckily I was!" Then, when he only looked at me, clearly waiting for an explanation, I told him about forgetting the deposit and, as I'd pretty much expected, he blasted me. "What are a few hundred quid in an envelope compared to your safety?"

"I know. But everyone's working so hard and the money was for charity. I would've felt awful if the money was stolen."

He leaned down and grabbed my shoulders. His hands were so strong I thought he might leave bruises. "Nothing matters as much as you. Nothing."

He let go of me then, quite quickly, and stood and stepped out of the way. And then I heard, as he already had, the footsteps running down the road towards us. The paramedics arrived first, two of them who immediately got down on their knees beside Gemma. One was short and stocky. He had close-cropped black hair and heavy glasses. I hoped he could see properly with them. The other was female. Pale, straight hair tied back in a ponytail. Tired blue eyes. She looked as though she had Nordic ancestors.

"Who found her?" she asked. "What do you know?"

Before I could say more than, "Um, I think she was attacked. Maybe strangled," the guy on the floor turned his head and looked at her. "She's alive. Get the body brace."

I was so relieved to have confirmation that she was still alive. "Will she be okay?"

He didn't get emotional. I suppose you couldn't when you

did a job like that. "Too early to say. We'll do our best."

And then the two of them brought a stretcher, oxygen, a medical bag. The lights of the ambulance were pulsing outside. While they were treating Gemma, Detective Inspector Ian Chisholm arrived with a uniformed cop. I was surprised. "Ian. What are you doing still working?"

His eyes moved swiftly between me and Rafe and then took in the scene. "I was working late on another case. The call came in, I was in the office." He looked at the paramedics. "She's alive?"

They both nodded. The woman said, "Looks like she's been strangled."

Then, to the three of us crowding around the edge of the door, she said, "Step outside, please." We did. It was cold. And I think the fear and shock made me even colder.

Ian looked at me, shivering, and took off his own coat and put it around my shoulders. It was like we were in a farce passing coats around. Except it wasn't funny. I was grateful for the warmth and I caught a hint of his scent on the coat. "What happened?"

I took a deep breath. Then, I related exactly what had happened, as I remembered it. How I had forgotten the cash in the Timeless Treasures chalet, returned for the money and then had seen someone running away from Gemma's chalet.

He didn't write anything down, merely watched my face. "Did you actually see them coming out of the chalet?"

"No. Just a black shadow at the edge of my vision disappearing between her chalet and the one beside it. I didn't see them come out of the door. I saw someone running away."

"Can you describe them?"

"I can do better than that. I know who it was." I explained

67

about Darren, how he'd been bothering Gemma and hanging around. "I saw him myself earlier today. He obviously got to Gemma after everyone had left and attacked her."

Ian was watching me carefully. "Lucy, you need to separate what you think you know from what you actually saw, heard, or experienced personally."

I felt like screaming. Who else could it be but Darren?

"Now, tell me exactly what you saw."

"Fine," I snapped. "One person. Just from the back. Wearing dark clothing. A man." Ian was right, I had to stick to what I absolutely knew to be true. "Probably a man. Fairly slim. It was just for a minute."

"Okay, that's good. Walk back over to where you were when you saw this person."

I looked at him, puzzled. "You mean stand in front of the Timeless Treasure chalet?"

"Yes. Exactly where you were when you saw this person running."

"Okay." I walked back to exactly where I'd been.

He said, "Rafe? How tall are you?"

"About six foot two."

"And I'm five foot eleven. Rafe, indulge me and run between the two chalets and disappear. And then I'll do the same. Lucy, look at where our heads are against the height of the chalet and see if that will help you determine the height of the person you saw."

I thought that was a really smart idea. I guessed that was why he was the detective.

Rafe cast a somewhat suspicious glance at Ian. But he obliged. He walked over and paused about two feet in front of where a narrow corridor separated Gemma's chalet from the one beside it that sold handmade wooden children's toys. He looked at me. "Ready, Lucy?"

I nodded. I tried to remember again that flash of movement I'd seen. Rafe ran between the two buildings like a moving shadow.

Ian said, "Well?"

"The man wasn't that tall."

"Okay. My turn."

He took the very position Rafe had. By this time the vampire had come around from the back of the chalet and was standing where Ian had been.

"Ready?" Ian asked.

"Yes."

He ran, exactly as Rafe had.

When he jogged around back the other side he looked at me. I walked over to join them.

"The person I saw was definitely not as tall as Rafe. About your height or maybe an inch or two shorter. I'm so sorry I can't be more specific, but they were running and it was dark." Anyway, I was certain it was Darren. I reminded Ian again that I'd seen the guy earlier today.

"And Gemma pointed him out to you?"

Why did he always ask the annoying question? "No. I saw him watching her. I know it was him."

"No. You don't. You're guessing." Ian stopped me before I could argue. "That's okay. You've done really well. Is there anything else you can remember? You said you might've heard something."

"It wasn't anything human, nothing like a cry. Maybe it was the door shutting. I don't know."

Rafe pulled the linen gloves out of his pocket that he

always seemed to carry, since he dealt in precious manuscripts all day. He slipped them on and then, only touching the top part of the door, he opened it and slowly closed it. The hinges squeaked.

"Yes." I nodded enthusiastically. "Yes. That's the sound I heard. Then, by the time I turned, the guy was running away."

Rafe stepped back and the paramedics wheeled Gemma out to the waiting ambulance. Her face was covered with an oxygen mask and her head and neck were encased in a neck brace. She lay so still I was frightened.

The three of us watched, quietly, as they put Gemma into the ambulance. Once it had driven away, Ian fetched my coat and Rafe's and then, a bit awkwardly, I returned his coat even as I grasped mine. We all hurriedly slipped arms into sleeves and buttoned up.

"I suspect you being here scared that young woman's assailant away. You may have been more help than you realize."

I nodded. It was pretty much what Rafe had said. Still, if I'd been more with it, perhaps I could have used the video function on my phone and filmed the guy running away. That would have been useful. I felt powerless and so angry. Someone I liked had been brutally attacked. "I hate that the attacker used one of Timeless Treasures' stockings as the weapon." They were not going to get away with hurting my friend with a stocking lovingly knit by one of the vampires. On that, I was determined.

Ian looked at the dark chalet where Gemma had been attacked. "I don't suppose you can identify who purchased that particular stocking?"

I'd already thought of that, and I shook my head. "It's a market. Most people pay in cash. We have a receipt book, obviously, but it's not like we're tracking stock like we do in the shop. I'll ask if anyone remembers selling that stocking, but it's a long shot."

"Do you have a surname for Darren?"

"No. But he texted her. Check her phone."

His gaze sharpened on mine. "Did she have it with her today?"

"Yes. She showed me Darren's creepy texts."

He shook his head. "I didn't find a mobile."

Of course. He'd taken it. Oh, how I wished I'd tracked that rat down and put my returning spell on him. I had to curl my fingers into my palms as I felt the electric pulses in my fingers. "We were only just getting friendly. She seemed so nice. She is nice." I would not start thinking or speaking of her in the past tense. "She's a teacher. She makes her own soaps and lotions. Why would he hurt her?"

He shook his head. "Hopefully, when she regains consciousness, she'll be able to help us."

More police began to arrive. I shuddered thinking that if Gemma didn't survive, this would be a murder investigation. But she was going to survive. She was young and strong.

Then, Ian touched my shoulder. "Try to get some sleep. And don't worry. You did a good deed tonight."

I smiled at him. But I didn't feel good. I felt awful. The holiday market was such a happy place. Nothing bad should happen here, not to someone I liked.

Ian didn't know it yet, and he probably never would know it, but he was about to get some very powerful help in finding out who had hurt Gemma.

CHAPTER 7

I got home to the smell of freshly-baked gingersnaps. Gran took one look at my face and said, "Oh, my poor love. What is it?"

"Rafe will explain. I have to call the hospital." They were unable to release any information since I wasn't a relative. I hated not knowing anything. I called Ian, finally, and he said she was still alive, which was a good sign but hadn't regained consciousness. That didn't sound like a good sign at all.

I slept poorly, worried about Gemma, and wishing I'd done more. I felt certain that I could have prevented the attack if I'd been a better friend.

I woke in the early hours of the morning, knowing I wouldn't get back to sleep. Nyx was a warm presence curled against me and I took comfort from her small, purring body as I stroked her and told her how worried I was. Nyx was a cat of few words, but great quiet empathy.

I got up about six, being as quiet as I could since Meri was sleeping in the other room. The vampires had left, though the pile of freshly-completed stockings proved they'd worked all night as usual. I made a pot of coffee. After the first few sips, I called the hospital again. Once more I was told there was no information available. I couldn't stand it. I'd found the woman strangled half to death last night, didn't I at least deserve to find out if she'd survived the night?

I knew that Ian had probably worked late into the night but I also knew that he was a caring and dedicated police officer. Also, he no doubt had a do not disturb function on his phone. I forced myself to wait until seven and then I called his mobile number.

He answered immediately, sounding perfectly wide-awake. Even so, I said, "I'm sorry to bother you so early. It's Lucy."

"I know. I have call display."

"Right. I've been calling the hospital and they won't tell me anything. How's Gemma?"

There was a tiny pause as though he was looking for the right words. My heart sank. Good news he would've told me right away. "She still hasn't regained consciousness."

My heart sank like a stone thrown into a still pond. Down and down and down. "What do you mean she hasn't regained consciousness? What does that mean? Is she in a coma?"

"I'm not a doctor, Lucy. It means she hasn't regained consciousness. I'm sorry. I'll let you know if there's any change."

"Ian, does she have some kind of protection?"

"She's in the hospital. She's safe."

"You don't know that. Whoever did this to her might go back and try and finish the job."

I heard him take a breath. He said, gently, "Lucy, I know you're worried. She's in good hands. And we're trying to find out who did this. The best thing you can do is try not to worry too much."

"Can I visit her at least?" I hated to think of Gemma lying there, all alone, with no one even to hold her hand and talk to her.

"That's a question for her doctors."

"But you could put in a good word. You could tell them that I'm her friend. She doesn't have any family close by. Her mother passed away last year. I don't think she has siblings, and she didn't seem close to her father. I'm her friend. I want to help."

"I know."

"You have to make sure that her ex-boyfriend doesn't get in to see her. I'm convinced he did this."

"At this point, no one is allowed to see her except doctors. I'll see if I can make an exception for you."

"Thank you."

I DON'T KNOW what Ian said, or how he managed it, but he called and told me I could visit Gemma on Saturday afternoon. I tried to put myself in her place and I imagined that I would want a friendly presence by my side.

No doubt they'd be trying to contact her father, though from the little she'd said about him I suspected he wasn't a very big part of her life.

I walked down to the market early, in time to see the forensics people finishing up. There was no note, or any kind of indication on the door of the shut up chalet that it would not be opening. I recalled that moment not so many months ago, when I had arrived at the door of Cardinal Woolsey's expecting to see my grandmother and been greeted by a note that said, "Cardinal Woolsey's will be closed until further notice."

Maybe it was better just to leave the chalet shut and locked with no explanation. Poor Gemma. I couldn't stop thinking about her.

Mabel and Hester were running the booth this morning, and, probably at one of the older vampire's urging, Hester had abandoned her usual black shroud and was wearing a pretty green jumper and jeans. For once, she seemed to be in a good mood.

Among the customers who came to Timeless Treasures were more than a few that I recognized from my shop. So, I was able to chat to them about the current projects and advise them on gift ideas. I was much better at selling completed projects than all the bits and pieces that went into actually making them. I could say, "Yes, I think your ten-year-old grandson will love that navy blue jumper," or "These extra long stockings are proving very popular this year. I think if you got them for the whole family, they'd be a nice heirloom purchase."

And they would be heirloom purchases. The vampire knitting club had outdone themselves. The little friendly competition seemed to have turned quite fierce when I looked at the amazing amount of work that had gone into some of them. I was hoping they wouldn't all sell out because I intended to keep a few for myself.

And, in between serving customers at Timeless Treasures,

I kept an eye on the sad, closed chalet that should have been Bubbles. In a way, it was as though the shop had never existed. The streams of shoppers glanced idly at a shut up booth and just kept walking. No one seemed particularly interested in why it wasn't there.

Until about eleven o'clock in the morning. That's when I saw him. It was the same guy I'd seen staring at Gemma the day she was attacked. He was in his early thirties, with a lean face, intense eyes, and shaggy hair that curled away from his face. He wore old jeans, a sweatshirt advertising a British beer and a black leather bomber jacket. He stopped in front of Bubbles, his hands in his pockets and rocked back and forth on his heels as though he might open it with the intensity of his gaze.

When that didn't work, he walked ahead a few feet, turned around and walked back.

Ian had accused me of jumping to conclusions. Sure, I had never been introduced to Gemma's ex-boyfriend, but I was making a not-terribly educated guess that this was him.

Had he returned to the scene of the crime?

A sensible woman would've ignored him, or pretended she didn't see him. I had already proved more than once that I was not a sensible woman. I was an angry one. Someone had hurt my friend and I had a very strong feeling it was him.

Before good sense could prevail, I'd stalked across the short distance and said, "Can I help you with something?"

He looked at me, somewhat surprised. Certainly, there'd been no friendliness in my tone, quite the opposite. If words were hailstones he'd just been pelted. He seemed a little taken aback by my cold hostility but he said, "I'm looking for the girl who's usually here. Do you know where she is?" I wasn't very good with English accents yet, but he sounded like a Londoner.

"Who are you?" I wasn't going to give him any information, not about Gemma or business or anything else, but I very much hoped I could get some information out of him. I tried to warm my tone. "She's not open today, but I can take your name if you like, and your phone number." And text it straight to Ian.

His brows drew together in a frown. His eyes looked intently into mine. "Is she okay? She sick or something?"

Oh, like he didn't know. I shrugged. "I have no information, but, as I said, I can take your contact details if you'd like."

"No. That's okay. I'll try again later." And then he ambled off.

I phoned Ian immediately. And, quickly explained what had just happened. "If you get here now, I bet you can catch him."

He said, "You want me to arrest someone because he hovered around Gemma's booth and said he'd come back later?"

"Can't you put a tail on him or something? Find out where he goes, and what he does?"

"Lucy, even if I had that kind of manpower, I can't have someone followed because you didn't like the look of him."

I understood he was right but the frustration was a burn in my chest.

"Fine." I said. "Sorry to trouble you."

"Lucy, don't be like that. You must see that I have to follow procedure. Hunches are great, I'm sure you're right and that is the ex-boyfriend who she thought she saw yesterday. It doesn't mean he attacked her."

"Well, somebody did. And he's the only one who's been hanging around looking interested."

We ended the call and I stood there, thinking. Maybe Ian couldn't do anything, but I had other friends who weren't constrained by the laws and rules governing the police. My second call was to Rafe. He sounded groggy when he answered and I realized with chagrin that I had woken him. "I'm so sorry. I didn't think you'd be sleeping. Never mind, I'll call you back later."

He yawned. "I'm awake now. What is it?"

I went through what I'd just seen and he agreed it was most likely Darren. "Do you want him followed?"

I'd been thinking about it, and I said, "I think I need to get inside Gemma's room. The police need evidence before they can do anything. Maybe we could find some?"

"That should be easy enough to do. Where's she staying?"

I told him she was staying in a budget hotel in Botley. He said, "I'll pick you up in an hour."

Rafe didn't mess around with rules or regulations. And he tended to be available, day or night. I liked that in a man. Or a vampire.

The hour wasn't quite up when the black Tesla slid to a stop beside me and I got in.

I didn't need to direct him, I suppose because he'd lived in Oxford so long. In about ten minutes we drew up in front of a very modest budget hotel. He said, "What room is she in?"

This was the moment I'd been dreading. "I don't know."

"That could be a problem."

"You always seem to slip in and out of doors. I thought you could get us in."

"I can, soon as I know which room she was staying in." He looked at me. "But I'm a vampire, not a magician." There was a significant pause. "Or a witch."

"I'm only a baby witch. And the last time I tried a spell I pretty much destroyed a circle of ancient standing stones. It's sort of thrown my confidence."

"Can you think of a human way you might find out the room number?"

I thought for a moment. "As a matter fact, I do."

I had a few paper bags in my handbag with the Cardinal Woolsey's logo on them. I'd brought them in case we needed extras at Timeless Treasures and forgotten to leave them. I pulled out an empty bag. Then, with a sigh, I took my knitting out of its tapestry bag. I carried an extra ball of blue chunky wool in the optimistic hope that I might one day progress to needing it. I slipped it into the bag and wrote Gemma's name on the front. I handed Rafe the bag. He raised his eyebrows at me. I said, "Go into the hotel, and tell the person at the front desk that you're leaving this for Gemma."

"And then?"

"Then, I'm going to go and pick it up, pretending I'm Gemma. The chances are pretty good that whoever's at the front desk won't remember one customer from another. And, even more likely, they'll write the room number on the bag."

He took the bag from me. "All right. But if this doesn't work, you'll have to resort to magic."

Oh I really, really hoped it worked. I was way too nervous that if I tried magic I'd end up shifting the architecture of

Oxford around. The way I was going, the dreaming spires could end up dreaming in Glasgow.

Rafe disappeared into the hotel with the bag and moments later he reappeared. He got into the car and drove around the corner until he found a place to park. He turned to me. "Would you like to get some lunch while we wait?"

"Why would you think about lunch at a time like this?" Not to mention, that I'd never seen him eat much food.

He smiled slightly. "I can hear your stomach grumbling. It would be good for you to eat something; you're going on nerves. Also, it's going to be pretty obvious, if I drop off a bag and five minutes later you come to collect it."

"Good point." And I *was* hungry.

We went into a Costa coffee shop and he bought some kind of a cold-pressed smoothie while I got a cheese and ham toastie and a cappuccino. He was right. I wouldn't do Gemma any good if I fainted from hunger.

After I'd finished my meal, he returned to the car and I walked back to the hotel and went up to the front desk. The reception area wasn't much to boast about. There was a coin-operated coffee machine, a rather sad plastic plant that needed dusting and a fake wood desk. Sitting behind the desk an older man was doing a crossword puzzle. He looked up when I entered. I tried to look confident. "Good after-noon. I'm Gemma Hodgins. Did anyone leave a package for me?"

He looked at me as though he'd never heard the words 'Gemma' or 'package' in his life and then, with a rumbling sound in his throat, turned around and looked on a set of shelves behind him. I could see my bag sitting there, but I held my patience while he picked up and put down various items. Finally, he retrieved the one I'd come for and handed it to me.

"Thank you."

I walked out feeling extremely pleased with myself. As I'd hoped, when Rafe left the package, they'd written Gemma's room number on the front of it. She was in Room 411 and I'd used human intelligence and cunning rather than magic to find that out. Once I was certain the man was deeply engrossed once more in his crossword puzzle I headed to the back entrance and let Rafe in. He carried a battered leather briefcase, like a professor might use and it made him look so respectable, who would question our right to be here?

This wasn't the kind of hotel where you had to use a key to get the elevator to work. Partly because there wasn't an elevator. There wasn't much security, either. We climbed up three sets of stairs and when we got to the top, I was puffing. Rafe, of course, was not. There wasn't a soul in the corridor, which smelled of cheap disinfectant. We got to the door of Room 411 and stood there. Then Rafe turned to me. "Lucy?"

I had seen him go through doors that were locked on many an occasion. But he merely looked at me with his eyebrows raised.

"I wouldn't have brought you if I'd known you were going to make me do all the work." I felt huffy and nervous. He crossed his arms over his chest and leaned against the wall looking at me.

I had practiced an unlocking spell, and, in fact, had helped save my mother's life by invoking it during a tense moment. But that was then. I wasn't sure I could do it now. Or, worse, I was afraid I'd split the hotel in two, or cause an earthquake.

"You can do it," he said softly and I tried to believe he was right.

I took a deep breath. I intertwined my fingers, closed my eyes, and as I recited the simple spell I opened my two hands. I think I held my breath. Then I heard the lock mechanism make a whirring sound. I turned the handle and pushed on the door and it opened as though I'd used my key card.

Like magic.

CHAPTER 8

*R*afe followed me inside as the door shut. "Well done."

I was ridiculously pleased with myself, but I played it cool. I looked around the room. "I want everything we can find about Gemma's ex-boyfriend. His name, his address, what he does, anything."

Rafe nodded. From the pockets of his overcoat he withdrew a pair of cotton gloves and handed them to me. I hadn't thought that the police might come here and take fingerprints, but he was right to take precautions. I took the gloves and slipped them on. He had a second pair for himself.

Before I did anything, I stood and looked around the small, shabby room. The space smelled like Gemma, somehow. A bit like her soap ingredients, like lavender and essential oils.

The double bed was neatly made, and covered in a cheap polyester throw. There were two pillows leaning against an imitation-wood headboard. A TV was bolted to the wall. There was a fake wood desk, a three-drawer dresser, a beaten up looking armchair, and a single bedside table. A tiny bathroom off the room completed the amenities.

Rafe looked at me. "What do you think? What do you feel? What do you sense?"

I breathed in deeply and closed my eyes. I knew he was right and I should call on my witchy senses. I had to trust them, to find a way to manage my powers without fear. I'd experienced similar feelings when I was learning to drive a car. I was supposed to be in control of a motorized vehicle that weighed several tons, even though half the time I was either stalling the car or accidentally going too fast, or too slow. But, I did learn to drive in the end. I could do this.

What was the room trying to tell me? I tuned into my intuition. "I feel sadness. I feel anger." I opened my eyes. "What I don't feel, is fear."

Rafe nodded and scanned the room. "So, she wasn't frightened of the ex-boyfriend. At least, not when she was last here."

That she'd been using this hotel room as a makeshift soap factory was evident in the number of boxes stacked in the corner. They were all neatly labeled with the varieties of soap, her bath salts and bath oils and creams. On the desk was a cutting board and several knives, plus the handmade paper she used to wrap things in. Like Timeless Treasures, I felt that she'd been caught off guard with the amount of success she'd achieved. She'd clearly brought extra stock just in case, but hadn't done all her packaging when she arrived. I could picture her there, in the evening, wrapping, labeling, packaging. Maybe with the TV playing in the background, or some music.

She'd hung some clothes in the wardrobe and a suitcase

sat in the corner. Her laptop had been pushed to one corner of the makeshift desk. Rafe looked to me. "Laptop?"

"I feel awful, going into her private things."

He quirked one brow. "You didn't mind breaking into her hotel room. Now you're going to be squeamish about searching it?"

"Okay, I don't always make sense. I'm just telling you what I feel."

"Remember that we are here with the purest of intentions. She need never know we've been inside her room, and anything we discover we use only to help Gemma and to get her justice."

I nodded. "You take the laptop." I thought I'd feel less intrusive going through her things. Besides, I was her friend, and another woman. If anyone was going through her underwear drawer, it was going to be me.

And I did. I went through each of her drawers carefully and methodically, and tried to put things back the way I'd found them. She wasn't the tidiest person, so I doubted very much she'd notice if things were slightly out of place. Her underwear drawer contained nothing but underwear. The middle drawer was stocked with T-shirts and sweatshirts. In the bottom drawer were two pairs of jeans and a pair of black trousers. Even though she had unpacked I still took the time to unzip her suitcase and check inside of it. At first glance, it appeared empty and then I noticed there was a separate flap. I ran my fingers inside it and discovered a file folder.

The minute my fingers touched it I felt an electric zapping. I pulled my hand out immediately because sometimes electric sparks shot from my fingertips without me being able to control them and I didn't want to set fire to whatever this was. I shook my hands for minute and imagined I was plunging them in cold water. That took care of the heat in my fingertips. I reached in again and this time I was able to take out the file folder. It was a well-worn, manila one. There were grubby thumbprints on it and pencil notations. I was no expert but it looked quite old. I glanced at Rafe but he was tapping away on the computer, a study in concentration.

I sat on the bed. I was glad I was wearing gloves as I set the file folder beside me and opened the cover. I don't know what I expected. Maybe a series of increasingly threatening letters from the unhinged ex. But this was nothing like that. It looked like the beginning of a novel. I began to read and then I thought the words sounded familiar. "Rafe."

He didn't look up. "Found something?"

"I don't know. Does this sound familiar?"

I began to read. The prose had a peculiar rhythm to it. The phrases were cold, and haunting. They described a man and a woman walking across a snowy landscape. I reached the end of the first paragraph.

Now, Rafe looked up. "That's the opening paragraph of the first volume of Chronicles of Pangnirtung."

I felt a funny bubbling sensation in the pit of my stomach. "I'm not reading to you from a novel. These look like old manuscript pages." The typewritten words had faded and the pencil scrawls had smudged over time. "Why would Gemma have manuscript pages from Chronicles of Pangnirtung?"

We looked at each other. Clearly we were both recalling the story that Rafe had told me about how her father had claimed to have written the fantasy trilogy.

He stood slowly and came over to the bed. He sat beside me, picked up the first piece of typewritten paper. He looked at the first page and turned it over and then he looked at the second one, studying it closely. I was going mad with impatience but I forced myself to stay quiet. Rafe was always slow and methodical and I knew that I would not rush him.

If I pestered him with questions I'd only slow the process down. After about what felt like an hour and was probably eight or ten minutes, he said, "This is very interesting. It's a very early draft with pencil corrections. I'd have to look at a copy of the published work, but I think this is slightly different. Maybe from before the manuscript was edited."

"Do you think it's possible that Gemma's father actually wrote the Chronicles?"

He looked at me but I felt that he was looking into the past. "I don't know. Anything's possible, of course. This could also be an elaborate hoax. He and Sanderson were friends at Oxford. He could've taken the draft and tried to pass it off as his own."

I looked at the pile of pages. The beginning of a legendary novel, lumped on a cheap, polyester bedspread in a shabby hotel room. "Or Sanderson could have?"

He tapped his gloved fingers against the open file folder. "Of course, Sanderson could be the villain." He ran a finger over the first page. "Provenance. It's all about provenance. Sanderson has the weight of history, success, and an entire industry built around these books. That's all stacked on his side. On the other side is a lone voice, a man who was discredited as a young man and whose claims were summarily dismissed when he first brought them nearly forty years ago."

"But why would Gemma bring this with her if she didn't somehow think that maybe her dad was right?"

He smiled, sadly. "Love can blind us to any number of faults. It's commendable that she believes in her father. But what do these pages prove?"

"You're the antique book specialist. If anyone could determine provenance it has to be you."

He looked at me and I could see the wheels turning in his brain. He didn't so much as twitch a muscle but I could feel his excitement. He relished the challenge of investigating this literary mystery. "One of the key exhibits in the Sanderson retrospective is the earliest known draft of the book. Sanderson himself has said it's the earliest draft. If we can prove that this one is earlier, Gemma's father would at least get a hearing."

His excitement was catching. Who knew a bunch of old typewritten pages could cause so much fuss? "The manuscript's not doing Gemma any good here in a suitcase. I think you should take it. Keep it safe. Find out what you can."

He nodded, slowly. "Yes, I think that's best. It's not safe here. Anyone could break into this room." He grinned at me. "Even you were able to manage it."

I punched him on the arm, but not very hard because I didn't want him dropping that precious manuscript.

"That's quite a find."

I thought so, too. "How about you? Any luck with the computer?"

He looked as though he'd forgotten all about his computer search. Then, after glancing over at the laptop, nodded. "There are some emails I think you'll find interesting."

The way he said the word 'interesting' had me getting to

my feet and walking over the open laptop and what looked like a list of her recent emails displayed on the screen.

He sat down in the chair, turned the laptop towards me and hit a button that brought up the first email.

It was from someone called Motorhead325. Rafe said, "The spelling's appalling. I don't know why they can't teach children to spell anymore."

"Probably because we don't have flogging, like in your day."

"Pity."

I started to read. I saw what Rafe meant about the spelling, it *was* appalling.

"I dont know what you think yer playing at. I thout you were the coolest girl, now I just think your a cold bitch. Why wont you talk to me? We have to talk. You have to talk to me. I luv you."

I looked up at Rafe. "Note to Motorhead, not the best way to a woman's heart."

He nodded. "That was only the first one." There were a string of emails and not only did the spelling get worse but they started to ramble. "Do you think he'd been drinking when he wrote these?"

"I couldn't say. Disturbing, though, aren't they?"

I nodded. Also evidence. "We don't know for sure these are from Darren, but who else could have written them?" I wished I could just forward the emails to Ian. He could find out who owned that email address. But I knew I couldn't. I could only hope the police came here to search her room. I had no idea what the legalities were if a woman was in a coma. I was certain of one thing. "Darren sounds unhinged and dangerous. If he left Gemma for dead and finds out she's alive and in the hospital, what's to stop him from going in and finishing her off? A few minutes with a pillow over her face? Everyone would think she died of her injuries."

"You don't trust the police and hospital staff to look after her?"

Did I? "I know they mean well. They're understaffed. They don't know what we know. I tried to tell Ian about the guy hanging around, asking questions about Gemma, and he said there was nothing he could do."

"In fairness to him, somebody hanging around asking where the proprietor of the shop is isn't particular criminal behavior."

"It is if he tried to kill the woman in question."

Rafe opened his briefcase, took out a memory stick and very quickly copied the file of emails onto it. I looked my question at him and he said, "In case they get deleted somehow. At least there will be evidence somewhere that these emails were sent. Hopefully, it's just a backup and the police will find this laptop themselves. Or be able to dig into her email account."

I brought my thumb to my mouth and began to gnaw on my nail, a horrible habit I have when I'm really stressed. I said, "I suppose I could tell Ian that Gemma showed me these emails."

Rafe put a gentle hand on my shoulder. "But she didn't. It's never a good idea to lie to the police."

"I know. I'm just so frustrated. I want to do something."

"One thing we can do is to put an informal watch over Gemma. I've got people in the hospital, connections. Between us, the members of the knitting club can find reasons to visit friends in the hospital. We'll do our best to keep her safe."

I nodded, feeling the weight ease off my shoulders. I knew I could count on Rafe and the other vampires. "Thank you."

He shook his head. "No. Thank *you*. Before you came along, we were all in danger of falling into lives of utter boredom. Since you've arrived in Oxford, there's never been a dull moment."

I knew he was being sarcastic, but he was right. There'd been one disaster after another since I'd arrived. Most of it wasn't my fault. But, some of it was. Flying standing stones, I had to take responsibility for. Maybe, my parents bringing curses from Egypt was partly my fault. But the rest? I put that down to bad luck and circumstance. I felt, sometimes, like I and Cardinal Woolsey's were at the epicenter of an earthquake of bad luck.

Rafe slipped the manila folder containing the manuscript into the briefcase. It couldn't have looked more innocuous. Then, after opening the door a crack and making sure there was no one in the corridor, we eased the door open and headed down the stairs. The scent of disinfectant and dust felt choking in my throat as I walked faster and faster. I just wanted to get out of this place. We had essentially stolen private property out of a hotel room. Even though we'd acted with the best of intentions, I'd feel a lot better when we were far away from here. I wondered if they had CCTV cameras. I glanced around guiltily. Why hadn't I thought of security cams? They were everywhere in England. I didn't see anything, but, as we slipped out the back entrance, I kept my head down. Not until we'd arrived at Rafe's car and were sitting inside it, did I express my fears that we might've been caught on camera.

He didn't look worried. "If anyone asks, a friend left something at the front desk for Gemma and, when you realized she wasn't going to be coming back for it, you went to the hotel and picked it up. The bag has Cardinal Woolsey's printed on the front of it. It's a perfectly logical explanation."

I looked at him suspiciously. "Wasn't it you who said one should never lie to the police?"

He started the car. "There are exceptions to every rule."

It seemed to me that Rafe lived by his own set of rules but I didn't feel like getting into an argument. He'd done me a huge favor. He was going to do me another one by investigating that manuscript we'd found in Gemma's suitcase.

CHAPTER 9

*B*y this time, it was after three o'clock and I decided I'd best put in an appearance in my own knitting shop. When I got there Meri was looking rather flustered, holding a smartphone as though she'd never seen one before, while two customers posed in front of the colorful wall of wool waiting for her to snap their photo. "I am sorry, which button is it?" she asked in her sweet, soft voice.

Oh the poor dear. I strode forward and said cheerfully, "Meri doesn't believe in mobile phones. I'll take the photo for you."

Meri sent me a glance of gratitude and I snapped the photo. The girls turned out to be from Italy and were going to put a picture up on Facebook of my delightfully English knitting shop. Since they'd made a sizable purchase, they were helping to keep my unique English knitting shop in business, which I appreciated.

When they'd left, Meri said, "I will never understand everything there is to know. How did the world change so much?"

I said, gently, "A lot happens in three thousand years. You're catching on fast. It's going to be okay."

"I hope you are right."

Since I tried to think of these difficulties as teaching moments, I got out my smartphone and showed her how to take a picture. I described the concept of the selfie, and she giggled. "Why would a person want to take their own likeness? It would be like a court painter making self-portraits all day long."

I loved her take on habits I no longer thought strange.

I showed her how I could connect to the Internet, use the phone to find my way around the city and even, astonishingly, make phone calls. She shook her head in amazement. "So much in such a small package. You are certain that machine is not inhabited by a trapped witch?"

"I'm sure." And I tucked the phone back in my bag before she could try and break it open in case one of our sisters was, indeed, trapped inside.

"I'll get you your own mobile. Once you practice, you will love it." And I'd start her with an inexpensive phone in case she tried to free the witch!

"Where's Violet?" The whole point of having my cousin as a second assistant was to prevent Meri from getting into difficulties.

"She went to get some coffee, but she won't be long."

I felt so bad that I hadn't seen much of Meri lately that I cooked her dinner upstairs in the flat. For once there were no vampires there. I think they were all still sleeping. The real work began when they were rested and refreshed, at around ten o'clock at night.

I invited Violet too, and she seemed surprised. "I want your help," I admitted.

"So long as we order pizza, I'm in."

I wasn't sure whether Violet really loved takeout pizza, or whether she was as afraid as the rest of the coven that eating food I'd prepared could be as disastrous as getting me to demonstrate a spell. Still, when Meri said, "What is this thing you call pizza?" I agreed that ordering it was a great idea.

Meri would learn about an essential food and I wouldn't have to cook. Win-win.

Once the three of us were sitting around the dining table eating pizza, I explained that I wanted a protection spell for Gemma. I didn't tell them I'd broken into her hotel room, obviously, or about the emails, but the man I was certain was Darren had been scary enough that they both agreed with me she needed protecting.

However, we hit a snag.

Violet said, "I'm not sure how to do a protection spell that won't prevent the doctors from doing things to her. Sticking IV drips in her and so on."

I put my pizza slice back on my plate. "You mean there isn't such a spell?"

"No. I mean if there is, I don't know it. I'll ask Mother. And Margaret." She picked a mushroom slice off her pizza and popped it into her mouth. "Could she drink a potion?"

"She's in a coma. How's she going to drink?"

"Right. Hmm. Let me do some research."

It wasn't what I'd hoped for, but I hadn't been able to find anything in my grimoire, either. Margaret and Lavinia would know if there was such a spell.

Meri had been quietly eating her pizza but now she spoke

up. "I can help you, I think." She hesitated, then removed her silver bracelet which was engraved with an Egyptian protection spell and offered it to me. "This was given to me by my priest. It has powerful properties to keep the wearer safe."

I didn't grab for the bracelet. "Meri, you were trapped in a cursed mirror for thousands of years. I don't think your bracelet worked."

She smiled at me, "Lucy. In all that time I did not die. And was reborn here, with you. The spell was, indeed, powerful. That is why I was never killed when the evil demon who trapped me destroyed so many of our kind."

I glanced at Violet, uncertain and my witch cousin said, "Well, it can't hurt."

I drove Gran's old Ford to the John Radcliffe Hospital that Saturday afternoon. As I made my way to Neurology I wished I had a magic spell that could make Gemma better.

I went to the nurse's station and, when I stated my business, the nurse on duty immediately called for a doctor. I waited for a few minutes and then a doctor came toward me walking quickly, as though he were always in a hurry. He was quite young and slim, and already balding. He introduced himself as Dr. Patek. "You are Gemma's close friend, I'm told."

Close might be pushing it, but if pretending our relationship was cozier than it was got me in to see her, then I was her BFF. "Yes. Her mother passed away last year and she has no siblings."

"So I understand. You were the one who found her?"

I swallowed as the awful picture of her lying there on the ground flashed on my inner eye. "Yes."

"She's in a coma. When you see her, you'll think she's sleeping, and in a way, she is. But it's very deep. However, we know that some coma patients hear and respond to friendly voices, you might even play her some of her favorite music."

"Do you know...will she be okay?"

He looked kind but he must deal with anxious friends and relatives all day. "It's too early to say. She was deprived of oxygen and we don't know for how long, and she probably hit her head. Her body is responding to the trauma and our job is to let her rest and help her heal."

"What can I do to help?"

"Talk to her. Hold her hand. I'm sure you know better than to refer to the attack. Speak about things you have in common, cheerful things."

He led the way into her room. Gemma was hooked up to a lot of monitors and an IV tube ran into her arm. Otherwise, she lay on her back, appearing to sleep peacefully. The marks had come out on her throat, angry and bruised. I touch my fingers to my own throat, feeling as though I were choking.

I felt a little self-conscious at first, when Dr. Patek settled me beside her in a chair. He stood at the end of the bed observing. I took her hand. We weren't the best of friends, but I went with my instincts. Her hands seemed cool and almost impersonal because, of course, she didn't return my grasp. I said, "Gemma, it's Lucy. I can't wait until you're feeling better and open your eyes. A funny thing happened at the holiday market, today." And then I recounted an incident where two men had both wanted the same sweater for their grandsons and, since there was only one, had decided to arm wrestle for the right to buy it. The match had been undertaken in a lighthearted manner and drew a small crowd.

The winner got his sweater and I'd taken the business card of the other man and promised to try and get him an identical one. I was fairly certain one of the vampires could whip him up one in a couple of days, though obviously I didn't share that with Gemma or the doctor watching us.

At the end of my story I glanced up at Dr. Patek and he nodded, gave me a thumbs up gesture and then quietly left the room. I just kept talking. I remembered the night in the pub and the way we had shared confidences as women do. I reminded her of how much fun we'd had that night and told her I was looking forward to lots more.

Then, when I was certain no one was looking, I slipped Meri's bracelet onto Gemma's wrist. "This will keep you safe," I whispered. "Blessed be."

CHAPTER 10

*I*t was a Saturday night and we'd all been working so hard, I decided we needed a break. I said to Meri, "Would you like to see a movie?"

"Movie. This is like the television?"

"Yes. Only bigger. And we'll go to the cinema, which is something you just have to do."

"All right, Lucy. How must I prepare?"

"Wear something comfortable. There's a funky art house cinema doing a showing of the first Star Wars movie. It's old, now, but I think you'll enjoy it." I had another brilliant idea. "Would you mind if I invite Rafe?"

"You must invite whomever you desire. It is your party."

"I wish everyone had your manners." I called Rafe and invited him along. After a pause, he said, "I can see why you want to expose Meri to this new experience, but why do you want me to come?"

"Because you are nearly as out of touch as she is. Admit it. You've never seen Star Wars."

"For good reason," said the cultural snob.

"Get over yourself. Everyone should see Star Wars. I'll even buy the tickets."

He agreed and the three of us headed to Walton Street to see a movie that was ancient to me, and would be blindingly modern to them.

We settled into the theater with popcorn and cold drinks and I had as much fun slyly watching Meri and Rafe as I did watching a movie I'd already seen a few times. When it was over, we walked to the café across the street for coffee and cake.

"Well? What did you think?" I was looking at Rafe but Meri spoke up.

"I was reminded of my homeland. The background looked so familiar." She sounded sad and homesick.

"That's right. It was filmed in Tunisia, I think. That's near Egypt, isn't it?"

Rafe said, "Egypt and Tunisia are separated by Libya, but not too far apart. The terrain is similar."

Honestly, sometimes being out with him was like dating Google.

"Meri, are you homesick?"

"Thank you, my health is very good."

"No. Homesick is when you wish you were back to where you grew up."

She looked so sad. "Everyone I knew is gone now."

"But the scenery is the same. The pyramids are still there." We'd all believed she'd be happier here with me and our local witches, but maybe that wasn't true. She sipped her espresso as though it took her whole attention. "Meri, would you like to go back to Egypt? You could stay with my parents. Pete, the Australian archaeology student works with them."

"I remember."

"You only have to say the word."

She smiled. "I would like that very much."

I had a sinking feeling I was going to lose another assistant, but I couldn't think about that now. "I'll talk to my parents and see what we can arrange. You'll get to fly on a plane. That will be another first for you."

"Thank you, Lucy."

Rafe still hadn't said a word about the movie. I turned to him. "You didn't seem at all bored during Star Wars." In fact, he'd laughed once or twice, a low rumble, and I'd definitely felt him jerk beside me in a few of the exciting scenes.

"It was quite entertaining," he admitted.

I forked up some more of my Victoria sponge cake. "They're doing The Empire Strikes back next week. Want to see it with me?"

"If you like," he said.

I hid my smile by stuffing my face with cake. He was hooked. My plan to teach him the best of modern American culture was working.

SUNDAY, after the market closed, Alfred and I started to close up, but I could see he was tired. "Go ahead. You've been on your feet for hours. I'll finish up."

He shook his head. "Rafe's orders. Until this maniac is caught, you're not to walk to the bank or home alone."

Of course, I was irritated by the high-handed way Rafe had gone behind my back and ordered bodyguards. I was also grateful to him, but it was annoying not to be asked—or at least informed that I had a protection detail.

"Fine." We finished locking up Timeless Treasures. I tucked the envelope of cash deep down in my bag and Alfred and I started off toward the bank.

We'd barely gone out of the pedestrian zone and onto George Street when a motorcycle zoomed up beside us. It was black. I didn't know anything about motorcycles so had no idea what kind it was, but there was a decal on it that caught my eye. It was about six inches long and featured a cartoonish image of a green rocket in flight. The words *Road Rocket* had been amended with a Sharpie to *Babe Magnet*.

The rider had on a helmet but when he lifted the visor I recognized the thin face and intense eyes of the guy who'd been asking questions about Gemma. "Wait. I want to talk to you."

I couldn't believe he was accosting me and I was very glad I had Alfred with me. He might not look like the toughest guy in a dark alley, but Alfred had hidden depths.

At first, I ignored the call and kept walking, but he pulled forward and when the sidewalk dipped he pulled in front of us. "Hey. Hold up a mo."

I had to curl my hands into fists so he wouldn't see the electricity zapping out of my fingertips. I felt I could zap him into a piece of charcoal just by shaking his hand.

He said, "Bubbles, the soap shop, it never opened all day. You must know what's happened to that girl who ran it."

"I already told you, I have no information."

I tried to walk around the bike, but he leaned out and grabbed my arm. His grip was strong. "I'm worried, all right? I know her. Somebody must know what's happened to her."

Alfred said, with steely menace, "Unhand that lady."

I was abruptly released. "No offense." He held up his hands as though he were being arrested. "I'm worried about a friend, that's all."

I'd had about enough of this stalker. My palms were stinging as I kept giving myself electric shocks. "Is your name Darren?"

His eyes opened wide. And then they narrowed. "What if it is?"

"Because, if it is, I can tell you that Gemma doesn't want anything more to do with you. You should leave her alone."

I wanted to add that if he'd hurt her he would be very, very sorry. He must've heard the venom in my voice. "I dunno what you're going on about. I didn't do nothing."

I really must get back to my magic. I wanted to turn Darren into a toad. I could picture his big, intense eyes set in a bulbous toad's body. I was shocked at my own viciousness. I'd never thought of myself as a vengeful person, but my new friend was in a coma and whoever had hurt her was going to pay. Darren was the most likely attacker, but I wasn't positive he'd done it and I wanted to be certain before practicing any transformation spells on him. I noticed, now, that he looked worried.

"Just tell me she's okay, will you? Then I'll go away. I promise."

I was tempted to tell him she was in a coma and might not survive. I wanted to see him blanch. But what if he thought she was already dead? Maybe finding out she wasn't would send him to the hospital to finish the job. I couldn't put her in worse danger. So, I shook my head. I wouldn't lie, but I wouldn't give him any information, either. I turned and began to walk away.

"I'll ask her dad. Maybe he'll give me the time of day."

When I still didn't answer, he yelled something very rude at my back. I felt my shoulders stiffen but I didn't turn. I took Alfred's arm so that he couldn't act on his instincts, which I could feel bristling beside me. I wondered if Darren had any idea how close he'd come either to being turned into a toad or dinner for a hungry vampire.

"Thank you for not eating him," I said to Alfred as we walked on.

He sniffed. "O positive. Doesn't agree with me."

Rafe called that evening, while I was showing Meri how to shop for flights using the Internet. I'd phoned my folks and we'd agreed that a trip in the spring would work for everyone.

He said, "I've got some interesting information about that project we were discussing." He had to be referring to the manuscript we'd borrowed from Gemma's room.

"Oh, yes?"

"I'd like to see you tonight. If I send a car for you, can you be ready in half an hour?"

I wasn't a package that needed to be picked up and delivered. "I can drive to your place. It's not a problem."

There was a tiny pause and I thought he might argue with me then, he said, "Fine. I'll see you when you get here."

I wondered why I bothered being quite so independent when I got into Gran's tiny car. It was freezing and I wasn't thrilled to be driving country roads at night. On the wrong side of the road.

As I waited for the windshield to defrost, I made sure I had the route pulled up on my map function in my smartphone. Once I had my courage up, the windshield clear and the interior a couple of degrees above frigid, I eased the car out of the tiny parking space and headed down the lane. The hardest part of the drive was navigating out of Oxford itself.

Oxford was not planned with heavy traffic in mind, and it showed. However, I navigated out of town without incident and once on the A44 I began to relax. No, not relax, I began to grow excited. Rafe wouldn't drag me all the way out there if he hadn't discovered something.

I arrived in a high state of anticipation. I parked the car in front of the imposing entrance to the manor house. I'd barely got the engine off and the car door opened before Rafe's butler-cum-manservant was standing with the great door thrown open, spilling out light.

"Good evening, Lucy," he said. "I'd have been happy to come and get you. It's tricky driving these roads at night."

He was so easy, so normal, and so human that I smiled. "I like to be independent, but sometimes I wonder why. I would've loved to have you pick me up."

He chuckled. "Next time."

I walked past him and he closed the door behind me. He waited for me to take off my coat and hand it to him. "You look frightfully cold. What can I bring you? Some hot tea? Coffee? Hot chocolate? Soup? Something to eat?"

"Thanks, William. A cup of tea would be lovely." That's how British I'd become.

"Rafe's in his office. I'll take you there so you don't get lost. And then I'll get the tea on."

We went down a long corridor and through a doorway to what I suspected might have been another wing or maybe even a stable block. I got a bit disoriented. William came to a thick, oak door and knocked. A brief word from Rafe and he opened the door and held it for me.

CHAPTER 11

*R*afe's office was the most modern part of the house apart from the kitchen. He worked at a large desk with leading-edge computers on it. On the opposite wall was a long counter that looked like a science lab with microscopes and powerful lights, a fancy camera. There were long, wooden cupboards that I assumed housed all the manuscripts and books he worked on because there was no clutter anywhere, though I spied the manila folder containing Gemma's pages on Rafe's desk.

He was sitting in front of a computer and he looked up. "Lucy. You found us all right?"

"Of course," I said, walking into the room. I left out the bit where the digital map and the computer voice giving me directions had saved my butt.

"I'll bring the tea," William said. "Rafe? Anything for you?"

Rafe shook his head. "Nothing, thanks." Then William left, closing the door behind him. Rafe said, "Come and look at this."

He pulled a chair over, close to him, and when I sat in it, we were side-by-side. So close our arms brushed. It was strange to sit so close to someone and not feel their body warmth. But he smelled as always, clean and of peppermint.

He looked to me. And then at the screen. "What do you see?"

It was a large screen and on it were pictures of two manuscript pages. I recognized one of them as coming from the manuscript we had taken from Gemma's hotel room. The other looked very similar, but the scribbled notes were in a different hand. I said as much.

He nodded. "Very good. In fact, the second page is from the earliest known manuscript of the Chronicles of Pangnirtung."

I looked at him, puzzled. "I thought you said that manuscript was on loan to the Bodleian and was at the Weston Library as part of the exhibition?"

"I did say that. And it is on display, minus a few pages which I have borrowed for scientific purposes."

I pressed my lips together against a grin. "I'm assuming it's an unofficial borrow?"

"Of course."

I didn't ask how he got the pages. Rafe had his ways.

He wouldn't have asked me to drive out here in the dark if he didn't have something interesting to tell me. I waited. He continued to stare at the screen and then said, "You have to understand that I have studied thousands of manuscripts. Often, it's a university or library wanting me to confirm that the gift they're being offered is, in fact, a genuine article. Sometimes a family member finds a manuscript and wonders if it might be of monetary, historical, or literary significance."

I nodded. I knew what he did for a living. Why was he telling me all this?

"One develops an instinct."

He turned and our gazes met. "It's hard to describe, but there are certain indicators in a genuine early draft of a manuscript and an imitator. Does that make sense?"

I nodded.

"I have studied the paper, the typewriter ink and the handwritten notations on each of these manuscripts."

I tried to control my excitement. "Can you tell which one was written first?" I really wanted Gemma's dad to be the author of the Chronicles of Pangnirtung. What a wonderful Christmas miracle that would be for her and her family. But, to my dismay, Rafe shook his head. "If there was a hundred years between them, maybe even ten, I could tell you which one was first. These were both written at approximately the same time. However, what's interesting, is the similarity of the paper. It's cheap copy paper, exactly what someone would've used forty years ago to draft a novel, or write the early draft of their university thesis."

"Forty years ago. So there were no computers then?"

He shook his head. "Oh, how young you are. There were, in fact, computers then, but not the personal computer. In the late 1970s, when this was created, most writers and students were still using typewriters."

"So, all we really know then is that one of them wrote the manuscript and the other copied it about the same time. Which we already knew."

He held up a finger. "Don't be so impatient." He pointed to the screen. "Take a moment, read the notations, and give me your initial impressions."

Even though he'd blown up the pages, it still wasn't so easy to read pencil and pen scratches on paper that was more than forty years old. Still, I did my best. When I'd finished reading as much as I could, he scrolled forward and there were two more pages for me to read. After the third page I did begin to see something interesting.

"The pages that appear on the left are suggestions to change a word, or reframe a sentence. They are specifically related to the language."

Rafe nodded, encouraging. I felt like a prize student he was proud of. "And the other?"

I looked at page on the right. "Those notes are reminders to check a source or, like here," and I pointed to where three different terms had been scribbled in the margin. "He's trying to decide what to call a particular creature, or dwelling."

"Very good. And what does that say to you?"

"Rafe, I run a knitting shop, I don't spend my life poking around ancient manuscripts. I don't know what it means."

"Let me ask you this. If I gave you the samples and said to you, which one is written by the author and which is the copy returned by the publisher's in-house editor, which would you guess?"

I nodded, slowly, understanding. "The one on the left seems more like editorial notes. The one on the right is more creative, I suppose."

"Excellent."

"So? Which manuscript is which? It makes sense that if they were such good friends the author might have given his buddy his manuscript to edit." I said, slowly, "That would be the one on the left."

"And the one on the right would probably belong to the true author since he was still making creative decisions."

"I agree."

"So? Which writer does the manuscript on the left belong to?" I felt butterflies of excitement dancing in my belly. I wasn't a bit surprised when he said, "The manuscript on the left is Sanderson's."

I let out a breath that almost sounded like a whistle. "So, if we're right, then Martin Hodgins is the real author the Chronicles of Pangnirtung."

"Yes. But it's a long way from suspecting he's the author to being able to prove it."

I got up and began to pace. William came in, then, carrying a silver tray. On it was a fine china teapot, one china cup and saucer, sugar in a Georgian silver bowl, and milk in the matching jug. On another delicate china plate was a selection of shortbread biscuits. I doubted the family at Buckingham Palace got served tea as beautifully presented. There was only the one cup on the tray and, in addition, a crystal tumbler of iced water with a slice of lemon floating on top, like a smile.

I thanked William and poured my tea. He left and I settled in a comfortable upholstered club chair in the corner of the room. There was a high tech reading light at my back and a leather ottoman in front. I imagined Rafe spent many an evening sitting in this very chair researching. Or, maybe, reading for pleasure.

"If what we believe is true, revealing it will destroy a man's life."

He began to pace. But stopped to turn and look at me.

"Not only a life. An entire industry. Think about the films, the comic books, the merchandising. The spinoffs from that series have been substantial."

I looked at him, feeling troubled. "So, if we prove that Gemma's father was the real author, then Sanderson will have to pay back all the money he's ever earned from the books."

Rafe laughed without any humor. "More than that. Any contract he signed was fraudulent. Martin Hodgins would be able to renegotiate every single contract, already knowing, as Sanderson didn't, what the monetary value of that series is. This could keep entertainment lawyers busy for years."

"Poor Sanderson." I didn't love what he'd done, but he'd lose everything. Probably even his teaching gig. I didn't imagine Cardinal College would want him when he'd been proven to be a fraud.

"If we're right, Sanderson is the one who destroyed a life first."

I sipped tea and nibbled a shortbread biscuit. "The trouble is, that Gemma's father has already been discredited. He was thrown out of Oxford as a plagiarist."

Rafe paused and looked at an oil painting of a battle scene hanging on the wall. I felt he was looking into the past. "If you can wound your enemy before the battle, he's that much easier to defeat."

No doubt he'd experienced that personally, maybe during the English Civil War, which I suspected was the subject of the painting he was still staring at. Still, I understood what he was getting at. "You're suggesting that Sanderson could have engineered the plagiarism charge against Martin Hodgins?"

"A man who would steal his best friend's novel and pass it off as his own wouldn't hesitate to discredit that same friend first."

I put my teacup down on the table that was perfectly placed beside the reading chair. "Rafe, what happens to an essay with plagiarized content? Would it still exist in some archive somewhere?"

He looked at me, frowning. "I imagine it's on file at the college."

"I'm just thinking, they were two students, in their early twenties. If Sanderson decided to do the dirty, he wouldn't be able to hire anyone. He'd have had to do it himself. Besides, he wouldn't want anyone to know what he was up to. He would have presumably stolen Martin's essay. Maybe he said, "Hey, I'm going to submit mine, I'll drop off yours at the same time." Martin had no reason to be suspicious. He was probably in the middle of writing a scene in his epic fantasy novel so he was grateful."

"Perfectly plausible."

I'd never gone to Oxford, but Rafe had. "Then what would Sanderson do?"

Rafe took a sip of his ice water. "He'd take the essay. He'd retype it on his own typewriter. Adding in sections plagiarized from other sources, or stripping out the footnotes that gave proper credit, and then he'd submit it as Martin Hodgins' work."

"You're sure they would be typewritten? The papers wouldn't be handwritten and there was definitely no computer then?"

He smiled at me. "Oh, you are so young. No, there was no

personal computer in the late 1970s, or at least nothing accessible to undergrads. Their papers would have been typewritten."

"Is it possible that Sanderson used the same typewriter to retype the essay and to copy his friend's book?"

He shrugged. "We're speculating here, but, as you say, they were students without a lot of resources. I think the chances are quite good."

I was warming to my theme, now.

"If we found that essay, would you be able to prove that it came from the same typewriter as that manuscript there on the left?"

"Yes." He took my wrist and pulled me gently out of the chair and towards the computer. "Look at the sections here. You see the way the G and the M are darker than the other letters. He used a manual typewriter. The way he typed using extra force on those particular keys is as individual as a signature. Also, the M is slightly crooked. I think we could make a compelling argument, if we could find that the supposedly plagiarized essay contains that same style of typing." He narrowed his eyes as he continued staring at the screen.

"You'll notice that the typewriter that was used for the manuscript on the right had an M key that was slightly crooked."

"It's not much though, is it? And, first we have to find that essay. If it still exists and hasn't been destroyed."

"Even if we could do all that, Sanderson could say his friend borrowed his typewriter. The weight of public opinion, history, and business is on Sanderson's side. We would need much more compelling evidence to launch a proper investigation into this."

I thought of Gemma lying unconscious in a hospital bed. I wanted to have good news for her when she woke. "There must be people still here in Oxford who were in school with Sanderson and Hodgins. I could pose as a graduate student doing my thesis on the very beginnings of the trilogy. I could interview their fellow students. See if they remember anything. People love to gossip and it must've been a juicy scandal at the time."

"Oh, it was. Oxford takes its reputation very seriously. And to have a former student claim to be the real author of the books, one who had been thrown out of Oxford for plagiarism, raised more than a few eyebrows."

I picked up my tea and Rafe walked back to the counter where the rest of the manuscript was laid out. He slipped his linen gloves back on he said, "Pangnirtung. The word is from the Canadian Inuit of Baffin Island. In the same way that Tolkien drew on Norse legends and his knowledge of old and middle English for his novels, so the author of the Pangnirtung Chronicles drew on the Inuit language and legends. There are references in Gemma's father's manuscript to books and sources that he drew on."

I stood up and walked over to stand beside him. "So, if he kept the manuscript, then he probably kept all those sources. Old books and maps and whatever he used for research."

"Exactly." He glanced over at me. "Has Martin Hodgins been notified of Gemma's condition?"

"I have no idea."

"Well, I think it would be worth our while to pay him a visit. Even if he's not at home."

"You mean, if he's not there, we can do a spot of quiet sleuthing?"

"That's exactly what I mean."

Maybe we were on a hopeless quest, but at least we had action steps we could take. I couldn't wait to get started.

$\mathcal{I}$ was a little nervous when I dressed to go and visit Professor Jeffrey Naylor. For some reason, I felt as though I'd been sent to the principal's office for doing something wrong. I was misrepresenting myself, pretending to be a grad student. I chose a somewhat obscure New England College as my pretend Alma Mater, only because I had a friend who'd taken classes there and I'd at least seen the campus.

I felt incredibly lucky that a guy who had known both Dominic Sanderson and Martin Hodgins now taught at New College. For probably the first time since I had opened Cardinal Woolsey's, I wore not one hand-knitted item. I had a superstitious dread that he might see me in a sweater and say, "Aren't you the young lady who runs Cardinal Woolsey's yarn shop?" Of course it was foolish, and I knew that, but anything I could do to settle my own nerves was a good thing.

I wore a tailored black skirt, black shoes, a long-sleeved white shirt and a tweed jacket that had been my grandmother's. When I looked at myself critically in the mirror, I thought it was the sort of get up a grad student might wear to visit a professor.

Rafe had brought me a digital recorder and showed me how to use it, and I also had a notebook and pen.

Professor Naylor was an excellent choice, not only because he'd gone to school with Dominic Sanderson and Martin Hodgins, but because he now taught a course called Oxford, Origins of Fantasy. The course was an intensive investigation into the works of Tolkien, C.S. Lewis, and Sanderson, all of whom had, supposedly, invented their fantastical worlds here in Oxford.

I was ushered into the professor's office right on time, at two o'clock in the afternoon, and I smiled to myself seeing him wear a very similar tweed blazer to the one I'd found in Gran's closet. With it he wore gray slacks and a white shirt with a tie. He seemed very old school. He was very thin, with wispy gray hair and faded blue eyes behind thick-lensed glasses. I gave him a bright smile and walked forward to shake his hand. "Professor Naylor. Thank you so much for seeing me today."

"Always delighted to help a colleague from across the pond." He motioned me to a hard-backed wooden chair on the other side of a battered wooden desk. As he settled himself behind his desk, I looked around the room. Floor-to-ceiling bookshelves were crammed with everything from obscure texts in Greek and Latin to the most modern fantasy novels. Among the pictures and posters on the wall was one of him standing with Professor Sanderson. From the age they both were, it looked as though the picture had been taken quite recently.

"I hope you don't mind if I record our conversation?" I

pulled the small recorder out of my handbag. "I don't take shorthand, you see, and I wouldn't want to miss anything."

He chuckled, indulgently. "Of course not, my dear. I just hope your batteries don't run out. Once I get talking about my favorite subject, I do tend to go on a bit."

The more he went on, the better I'd like it. Especially if he dropped interesting tidbits about the past into my lap. I smiled and said, "I find it fascinating, too."

I'd taken a crash course in Sanderson's work from Rafe, read the first couple of chapters of the first book, and poked around the Internet. If Professor Naylor quizzed me more than superficially, I'd be revealed as the fraud I was. However, the professor had no reason to distrust me and, fortunately, didn't ask me any searching questions. I took a deep breath. I clicked on the recorder and pointed to the picture on the wall. "I see you and Professor Sanderson are still friends."

He looked quite pleased at my initial comment. He puffed up with pride. "You've done your research. Yes, indeed. Dominic and I go back to our student days. We're all very proud of him, of course. Although, I have to say, I always knew he'd go places."

"Really? What were the early indications of genius?"

He sat back and steepled his fingers. It was a gesture I was intimately familiar with, as my dad took that pose when he was about to lecture. "We studied old English together. Dominic ended up with the top mark in the class." He opened his mouth, shut it, and then shook his head. "Well, he had some competition, but..." He shook his head, again. "But that's another story."

Oh, no, *that* was the story I wanted. "If you're talking about his friendship with a student named Martin Hodgins,

I'm very interested in that. Part of my research is about influences, both good and bad, that shaped the writer." Rafe and I had come up with that line as a way for me to pry into old scandals.

A gleam, almost like greed, glittered in his eyes. I thought, *You old faker, you love a good gossip.* And so I looked at him, as wide-eyed and innocent as I knew how.

He took his time, gathering his thoughts. "It's not a nice story. But it has almost mythical elements to it. The man of genius, the friend torn apart by jealousy who tries to steal his fire. Really, it had all the makings of a Shakespearean tragedy, with a good dose of farce."

Not so farcical to the girl currently lying in a coma.

"You must've known them both very well. What was their relationship like?"

"Sanders and Hodge? You couldn't have found two young men who were closer, I mean in a scholarly way, of course. That's what made it so sad. Martin Hodgins was intense, a dreamer. Half the time he seemed to be in his own world. Nowadays, I think we'd suspect he was somewhere on the spectrum. You'd pass him in a corridor, speak his name, and he'd walk on as though he hadn't noticed you. I used to wonder if I'd offended him, until I realized it was just his way. He really hadn't noticed me. He was so engrossed in his own thoughts."

The image fit nicely with a genius who was so busy creating his fantastical world that he lived there in his head.

"Dominic, on the other hand, was more genial, more gregarious. They roomed together, I believe, their first couple of years at Oxford. Then, they moved into their own lodgings, but still you'd see them together most of the time. There were students, and plenty of them, whose only goal in school was to get high marks. And then there were the ones who genuinely came to Oxford for the love of learning. I flatter myself as I was in the latter category, and certainly Dominic and Martin were. That's why it was such a shock, you see."

He shook his head and stared intently at his steepled fingers. "None of us saw it coming. Martin wrote brilliant essays. They weren't always particularly well researched, and, if he had a flaw, it was to range away from his topic and bring in very obscure references, but one couldn't deny he was brilliant."

"Really? How so?"

Professor Naylor took his time before answering. "He had some astonishing theories about Beowulf. Used to talk about this creature of Old English mythology as though he were a friend, a person whom he knew and understood. As I said, he was always slightly odd. Anyway, the end of term came, and we handed in our essays.

"We went out for a drink, and I could see he was troubled about something. He seemed even more withdrawn than usual and muttered into his beer. He was never the life of the party but on that occasion he was an absolute drip."

"Do you have any idea what was troubling him?" I was getting a picture of an intense young man who was more interested in mythological creatures than living, breathing humans.

He shook his head. "At the time, of course, I put it down to bad temper or lack of sleep. I'd have said girl trouble, but I don't think he ever had any girls. Now, of course, in retrospect I can see that he was troubled by his actions."

"And by that you mean...?"

"Well, by the time we came back from the term break, it was over. Hodge's essay was clearly plagiarized. The rumor was that it was actually quite brilliant, and he hadn't even needed the extra research that he'd lifted, verbatim. It was a sad affair."

I felt anger burn in my belly. I didn't even know this man, but I was increasingly convinced that justice had not been done. "Did he try to defend himself at all?"

He looked at me, and through the thick lenses of his glasses his eyes were magnified almost like insects. "Oh, yes. He claimed he hadn't done it. He claimed his essay had been tampered with. But, of course, there was no proof. He had no idea who would've done it. His defense didn't make any sense. And so he was sent down. As far as I know he never did finish his degree."

"That's awful," I said.

"Sadly, it was just the beginning. The following autumn Dominic Sanderson sold his trilogy. Well, rather, he acquired an agent who sold the novels to a very good publisher. He chose well. His agent was also young, and beginning his career. They've made each other, in some ways."

I remembered the man who'd set rules for Sanderson's book signing. "So, he still has the same agent?"

"Oh, yes." He chuckled. "You don't fire the man who's brought you lucrative film deals and merchandising and I know not what. He definitely still has the same agent."

I thought to myself that poor agent also had some bumpy seas ahead. But then, Charles Beach must already have weathered those. I tapped my pen against my notebook. "When did his former friend, Martin, come forward and claim that he'd written the books?"

He looked at the ceiling. "Let me think. It must've been when the books were first published. They were modestly successful from the very beginning and then the fame grew and grew. I would say the books had been out about six months, when, all of a sudden, Hodge came forward and claimed that he, not Sanders, was the real author."

"What did Dominic Sanderson do? His former friend claimed that that book was his? It must have been a terrible shock for him."

"Oh, it was. He was dreadfully upset."

"Had they stayed in touch, after the plagiarism?"

He looked and me and squinted his eyes, as though trying to remember. "I don't know. I don't think so. Dominic was a stickler for following the rules. I believe he dropped Martin after he plagiarized that paper."

"Had you known," I asked, "when you were all studying Old English together, had you known at that time that Dominic Sanderson was writing novels?"

"Oh, goodness, no. No. He kept it very quiet. I suspect Martin probably knew. Because, of course, they spent so much time together. Dominic told me, afterwards, that made it even harder for him, knowing his former friend with whom he'd shared so many of his ideas about the book would then try and claim he had some right to it." He shook his head. "Dominic was devastated."

I'll bet he was.

"Was there any kind of investigation? When Martin Hodgins came forward and claimed the books as his own?"

"To be honest with you, I think he'd already begun to drink. Simply because of the success of the novels, Hodge got some air time. I saw him interviewed on television and heard him on the radio, but, truly, I was humiliated on his behalf. He rambled, kept quoting Beowulf for some odd reason. I'm afraid the media made rather a mockery of him. Naturally, Dominic Sanderson denied the claims. He said he had talked over some of his ideas while he was writing the books, as one does with a friend. His agent made the very first draft available to any journalist who cared to examine it."

"What about Martin Hodgins? Did he have any evidence for his claim?"

"He kept saying he did, but then he never brought it forward. It was as though he simply couldn't find his supposed manuscript. Of course, the damn thing never existed. I suspect he was eaten up with jealousy and, very likely, psychologically troubled."

"Whatever happened to him, do you know?"

He shook his head. "He disappeared quite quickly after he got nowhere with his absurd claims. He was a five-minute wonder. I've never seen him since. No. No idea what happened to him."

I felt Martin Hodgins hadn't had a fair hearing. Maybe it was wishful thinking on my part, because I wanted Gemma's father to be more than a drunk and a literary laughing stock.

"What about the essay? That plagiarized essay? What happened to it?"

His eyes sharpened on my face. It was the first time I was aware of even a hint of suspicion about my motives in meeting with him. "Why on earth would that be of interest to you?"

I imagined grad students researched their way down all sorts of blind alleys, so I shrugged. "I thought I might look at how the influence of his friend, during those early years at

Oxford, might have affected Sanderson's work. It's just a vague idea at the moment."

His suspicion disappeared. Now, his eyes twinkled and he looked fatherly. "Looking for a fresh angle, I see." He nodded. "It's what you need to get any decent funding these days. I must admit it's unusual. I don't think anyone's studied the relationship between Sanderson and his closest friend and rival in his undergrad years."

I nodded, grateful. "Exactly. Especially as his book came out so soon after Dominic Sanderson graduated. He said he'd talked his ideas over with his close friend. I'm curious if I can find anything that might be seen as an influence on the author's work."

He said, "I wish you luck. I doubt you'll find anything useful, but you never know. The paper would be kept in physical copy, of course. It was written before computers."

"Any chance I could see the essay?"

"You'd have to be a student of this college."

I looked suitably disappointed. Then, in order to maintain the fiction that I actually was a grad student, I asked some questions that Rafe had helped me prepare about Sanderson's influences. Professor Naylor was more than happy to oblige me and pontificated at length.

When he finally wound down I said, with my most winning look, "Isn't there any way I might obtain a copy of Martin Hodgins' essay?"

I could tell that he wanted to impress me. "I'll see what I can do. Give me a call tomorrow. It won't be the original, of course, but I might be able to obtain a copy."

I rose. "That would be amazing. I can't thank you enough for your time today." I held out my hand and he stood up and shook it. "I wish you good luck in your thesis, my dear. And I hope you enjoy your time in Oxford."

"Thank you so much," I said, switching off my voice recorder and dropping it into my bag, along with the notebook that had very few notes written in it.

As I left his office I breathed a sigh of relief. I'd managed to impersonate a student and had obtained some pretty interesting information.

CHAPTER 13

*R*afe was waiting for me when I got back to the shop. I made him wait while I checked in with Meri and Violet. The shop was running so smoothly I wondered why I bothered to come and work at all.

Violet reminded me that the solstice celebration was next week and I developed a sudden and profound deafness.

I said to Rafe, "We can't go upstairs, the knitting factory is going full force up there."

"You can tell me what you discovered in the car. We're going on a road trip."

I felt like a super sleuth, undertaking two scouting adventures in one day. "Are we going where I think we're going?"

He shook his head at me. "I imagine so."

"I'll check in with Gran and be right with you." I ran upstairs and saw that the knitters were going full force. It was a pleasure to watch those needles fly and see exquisite creations appear almost like magic.

Having confirmed that Mabel would carry down the latest batch of knitting to the market and would bring back the bank deposit, I was free to go. "You've been working so hard, lately, dear. It will do you good to get out for a drive."

I ran to the bathroom and brushed my teeth and freshened my makeup. I swapped my fake grad student outfit for a super-sleuth cat burglar getup consisting of black skinny jeans, a pair of black running shoes, black T-shirt and black hand-knitted pullover. I added black gloves and a woolen hat, also black, that would keep my ears warm. I could also tuck my long, blond hair up into it in case there was any breaking and entering required.

I brought my bag along with me so Rafe and I could listen to the tape of my interview while we drove.

He looked slightly amused when he saw me dressed all in black, but there wasn't much he could say since he was also dressed all in black. Though, with Rafe, it was his usual look. He was not one for bright colors.

I thought for Christmas I might get him the most garish Christmas sweater I could find. Something in red and green with a Rudolph nose that lit up, just to see if I could get him to wear it, even for a minute.

He'd parked the Tesla in the lane behind the entrance to my flat, so we were on the road in no time.

"My interview went so well," I exclaimed, too excited to wait for him to ask the questions. "Professor Naylor is so thrilled that he knew the famous Dominic Sanderson when they were young, and that he knew all about that scandal, I bet it's the most exciting thing that's ever happened to him. He kept calling them Sanders and Hodge, their college nicknames, I presume, so I'd know they were tight."

"Like many professors, he teaches about genius rather than possessing it."

I felt slightly miffed on behalf of my parents. "Professors can be brilliant, too."

"They can. And teaching is a fine and noble profession. But, there's an expression you've no doubt heard: Those who can, do. Those who can't, teach."

I looked at him sideways. "You teach."

He slid his gaze sideways right back at me. "Yes, I do. I can't invent the brilliant manuscripts I value and preserve, I can only appreciate them and share my knowledge so that others may appreciate them, too."

"So we're agreed, then, that teaching is a good thing."

He chuckled. "We are. Now, stop arguing and let's get on with the interview. What did you discover?"

I jumped right to the chase. "Guess who thinks he might be able to get me a photocopy of a certain plagiarized essay? I'm phoning him tomorrow."

"Very impressive. What else did he say?"

I pulled out the recorder and played the interview for Rafe. I was pleased to hear it myself because I'd been so caught up in thinking how I might ask pertinent questions and worrying that he might ask me something about Sanderson's work and catch me out as a fraud, that I hadn't been able to relax and actually listen properly to what he'd been saying.

Neither of us said a word until the interview drew to a close. I asked, "Well? What are your impressions?"

He breathed in and out slowly. Rafe was not a man who ever rushed. Certainly not to judgment. "That sounded like a story he's told so many times he believes it."

I raised my eyebrows in surprise. "You mean he's lying?" That hadn't occurred to me.

He shook his head. "No. But he's recalling events from forty years ago. Sanderson's now a famous novelist. Naylor makes his living teaching his work. His chummy, anecdotal recollections fit in well with the mythology that Sanderson has helped to create around his own work."

I nodded. "You're right. Even to the point that he suggested that Martin Hodgins might have been mentally ill."

"Hodgins didn't do himself any favors when he first brought the claim. Professor Naylor was right. In interviews he did ramble. He didn't come across as credible, which made him very easy to dismiss."

I turned in my seat to look at Rafe's profile. It was clean and sharp. If I ran my fingertip down the bridge of his nose it would be dead straight. Naturally, I didn't. "Are you starting to think that maybe Martin Hodgins did plagiarize that essay? And Sanderson is the real author of the Chronicles?"

I was profoundly disappointed by this. I liked our quest to prove that Gemma's father was a literary genius who'd been unfairly maligned and had his life's work stolen from him. If Rafe was going to side with Sanderson, I wasn't sure I could complete this quest on my own. But, to my relief, he said, "No. There's a very real possibility that Martin Hodgins is the genuine author. Hopefully we'll know more soon."

"What are we looking for, exactly?"

"These manuscript pages that Gemma had, they came from somewhere. I'm keen to find the rest of the manuscript. I'm also hoping that Martin Hodgins still has the source materials that he referenced. Even better, if he's scribbled in the margins. If he can help us make the connections to where he got some of his ideas from and how he came up with place names and character names and so on, he'd be able to make the arguments he seemed unable to make four decades ago."

"Yes. Maybe he didn't have anyone on his side and then started drinking, which made everything worse for him. However, the best way Sanderson could have proven beyond any doubt he was the author was to have written another novel. Why hasn't Sanderson put out another book in forty years? He presents the world with an astonishingly brilliant and compelling fantasy trilogy in his mid-twenties and then never writes another thing? Why does Sanderson stop?"

"Because, as he's said in interviews, he felt he'd said what he had to say in the trilogy." Rafe glanced over at me. "Or, he never wrote the books in the first place."

An idea hit me, so exciting that I jumped up and down on the seat. "What if Martin Hodgins has been secretly writing all these years? Maybe he's got a whole bookshelf of manuscripts?"

"I wouldn't get your hopes up. I suspect your friend Professor Naylor was right and he did take to drink. I think his best friend's betrayal and the theft of his work probably broke him. Because, of course, your argument works both ways. If Martin Hodgins wrote the Chronicles, why has *he* never written another novel since?"

We cruised along the M40 motorway toward Crawley and I reached for the water bottle in my bag. I'd talked so much today, I had a dry throat. Still, I didn't remain quiet. "That's so sad. His whole career was stolen from him. And all the books he might've written in the last forty years, gone, because his closest friend betrayed him."

"Yes, I think Professor Naylor got it right. This is a story of

Shakespearean tragedy and farce. It's just that the characters are reversed."

"So, we have to put literary history right."

"Exactly." We turned onto the M25 and traffic grew heavy.

"Where are we going, anyway?" I'd seen signs to Crawley, but Gemma hadn't mentioned that her father lived there, too.

"Balcombe. It's a small Sussex village, a few miles from Crawley."

Interesting that the father lived close to his daughter. I wondered if they'd grown closer since she'd lost her mother. They were clearly friendly enough that he'd given her some of the manuscript, and she'd come to Oxford believing he'd written the Chronicles. I wondered what she'd intended to do with those pages. "Martin Hodgins is only sixty-five. I believe once he gets his reputation back, he'll get a whole new lease on life."

"I hope you're right."

I hoped so too.

We drove into the village center, with a strip of shops and, above them, tidy looking homes. Rafe said, "He lives outside of town, on a housing estate." I had a feeling that people lived on housing estates weren't exactly well-to-do. As we turned into the road, an emergency vehicle sounded behind us and Rafe pulled over to let a fire engine pass in a blur of red.

I continued thinking about Martin Hodgins. "I just hope Gemma recovers. Getting fame and fortune and his reputation back will mean nothing to him if he loses his daughter."

"There's no reason to despair." He reached for my hand. "Try to stay positive."

I knew he was right. He pulled over again to let another fire truck scream by, followed by an ambulance. We carried on in the wake of the speeding emergency vehicles. I didn't say anything, and I tried to ignore the feeling of doom that seemed to be crawling up my esophagus. No, Martin Hodgins couldn't be this unlucky.

Could he?

We couldn't get down the road where Martin Hodgins lived. It was blocked with emergency vehicles and trestles had been set up. A uniformed police officer stood there, moving the barricade to let the emergency vehicles through, but blocking the road to any other traffic.

I said, my voice sounding small, "It couldn't be Martin Hodgins, could it?"

"I don't know." But his tone was curt and I was fairly sure he thought, as I did, that our trip here may have been in vain.

Rafe got out of the car and walked up to the uniform. "We planned to visit Number 33. Martin Hodgins. Is he all right?"

The officer glanced back and then back at Rafe. "I'm very sorry sir. The fire started in Number 33."

I could see the blackened stone, the firefighters were pouring water into the windows and open door, but the smoke was still gushing out. And then I noticed a gurney with a blanket covering a body-shaped lump, outside on the sidewalk in front of the remains of Number 33. Two paramedics loaded the gurney into the back of the ambulance, but there was no hurry to their movements. And when the ambulance drove away, it didn't put on its flashing lights or the siren.

Rafe got back in the car and we drove back the way we'd come. I turned to look over my shoulder, out the rearview window, and watched as the same police officer Rafe had been speaking to, moved the barricade out of the way so that the ambulance could make its somber journey.

I felt like crying. I knew that super sleuths and cat burglars didn't usually melt into tears at the first sign of trouble, but I was devastated. Gemma was in a coma, her father was dead, his home burned to the ground and his life's work stolen from him. The manuscript pages we'd hoped to find, the source materials, they'd all be burned to ash. How could the tragedy keep continuing? They'd had forty years of bad luck. I'd hoped for a Christmas miracle and instead, when Gemma woke up, it would be to more heartbreak.

I glanced over at Rafe and his jaw was set in a hard line.

My initial shock was punctuated by questions. What had happened? That was my first question. Had the fire been an accident? How could one man be so unlucky in a single lifetime? But if it wasn't an accident, then the fire was deliberately set. And who would want to go after a broken man whose life had been stolen from him?

The image of Darren rose up before me. Could he have come to see Gemma's father? Had he had violence on his mind?

Rafe asked if I wanted to stop and get coffee or a meal or something but I didn't. I wanted to get back home. I felt a strange sense of urgency, that I should go back to Oxford and protect Gemma. That feeling was so strong in me, I willed the car to go faster even though I kept my mouth shut. Rafe was an excellent driver but I think some of my anxiety communicated itself to him. He glanced over at me. "The police have her under surveillance, you know, there are always doctors and nurses surrounding her, and some of the vampires are keeping an eye on her, too. Gemma is as safe as she can possibly be."

I nodded. But still, my hands gripped and twined around each other in my lap. For once, I actually wished I had my knitting with me so it would give my restless hands something to do, and my restless thoughts something to focus on.

"The last thing Darren said to me, when I wouldn't give him any information about Gemma, was that he was going to see her father." I could have kicked myself for not telling Ian, or Rafe, but I'd only been thinking of Gemma and hoping he'd just go away.

I have said that Rafe was an excellent driver, and he was, but at my words the car swerved slightly as though he'd lost his concentration. "You saw Darren? The man who's been harassing and stalking Gemma? The most likely suspect in her attempted murder?" He sounded angry but he got that way when he was worried about me.

"It wasn't my idea," I said, indignant. "Alfred was with me. He can tell you exactly what happened. We were accosted by Gemma's ex as we were leaving the market. He kept asking questions about Gemma, how was she and where was she and when I wouldn't answer, he grabbed my arm." I recalled those moments vividly. "If I hadn't hustled Alfred away pretty quickly, there wouldn't be much left of Darren right now."

"Good for Alfred."

I knew he didn't really mean that. Rafe believed in peaceful coexistence between our two species; he was also very protective of me.

We drove back the way we'd come. Traffic grew busier as we approached Oxford. It began to rain. "Do you think

Darren killed Martin Hodgins? And then set the house on fire to cover up his crime?"

"I don't know. Somebody strangled Gemma and left her for dead. He's the most obvious suspect. According to what he told you, he planned to visit her father."

"Maybe he turned up and Martin Hodgins didn't know about his daughter's condition. Darren might've thought her dad was lying. Maybe, he didn't mean to kill him. He was just going to rough him up a little to get the truth out of him, but he went too far, like he did with Gemma. He seems like a guy with a lot of anger in him."

Rafe didn't answer me and after a minute I looked across at him. "You don't like my theory?"

He considered my words. "It's a theory. But it's not the only one."

We had a long way to go and only the two of us in this quiet car. I said, "Okay. Let's hear some of the other theories."

He let out a slow breath. "We know that Martin Hodgins had lost everything. His reputation, a budding career, possibly the ownership of his brilliant fantasy series, and his family. Perhaps he saw the fortieth anniversary retrospective of his old enemy's brilliant success. Perhaps the hospital called him and told him his only child was in a coma. It was too much for him. He may have taken his own life."

"Oh, no."

Rafe smiled grimly. "With his fascination for ancient myths and rituals, he might've liked the idea of creating his own funeral pyre. He may have lived in obscurity, but he was going to go out in a burst of flame."

I considered his theory. It wasn't bad. A shiver went over my skin. "Or, less heroically, if he was indeed a drunk, maybe he was also a smoker. He had too much to drink and fell asleep on the couch with a lit cigarette." It was a sad way to end but not as uncommon as one might wish.

"Or, someone else murdered Martin Hodgins."

"But why?"

"I don't know. Perhaps, after all these years, Mr. Hodgins decided to have another attempt at proving his ownership of the manuscript? His old friend Sanderson had already eviscerated him professionally, perhaps he decided to finish the job."

"That stuffy old professor? I could see him stealing intellectual property, but killing someone?" I imagined Professor Sanderson with a weapon. Maybe bashing his old friend over the head and then setting fire to his home. I couldn't believe it. "I've never killed anyone, but I wouldn't think it was that easy to do."

"Easier than you think, if the motivation is there."

I shivered again.

He looked at me. "Try and relax."

I would relax if I wasn't so busy being stressed out and anxious. He cast another glance my way, then flipped on his Bluetooth and called Alfred, who answered immediately. Rafe said, "Is someone keeping a close eye on Gemma Hodgins?"

"Of course," Alfred said. "Mabel and Clara are both at the hospital now. Mabel's posing as Gemma's grandmother and Clara as her aunt." He was on speakerphone so I heard every word. I asked, "But how did they get in? Visiting was supposed to be limited to close relatives and friends only."

"I believe your cousin Violet helped get the documentation."

Nice work, Vi.

Rafe said, "Get a message to them. They are not to leave her side for a second."

"What happened? Has there been another attempt?"

"No. But her father just died under suspicious circumstances."

Alfred didn't waste time on chitchat. "I'll make sure they get the message."

"Good. Also, I believe you had an altercation with a young man who accosted Lucy? She says his first name is Darren."

Alfred made a sound that, I thought, was a growl. "Yeah. I remember him. Nasty little O neg."

"Can you find out where he is? I know it will be difficult to track him without a surname, but do your best."

"Don't worry, Rafe. I already tracked that little punk. I wasn't having him come near Lucy again when I wasn't around to protect her. No man should ever treat a delicately nurtured female that way."

I reminded myself that these vampires were hundreds of years old so their sexism came naturally. Besides, I wasn't averse to a little protection, whatever the motivation behind it.

"Where is Darren now?" Rafe asked.

"He left Oxford, that's all I know. On a motorbike. Nasty, noisy thing. He took the M40 headed toward London."

Rafe and I shared a glance. It was the same road we'd taken. It might lead to London, but it was also the road one took to get to Balcombe. "When did he leave?" Rafe asked.

"Last night. Latish."

"Excellent work, Alfred. Thank you."

And then he rang off. Rafe looked over at me. "So, Darren

took the same road we did when we went to visit Gemma's father."

I didn't want to jump to conclusions, even if they were obvious. "Yes, but that road goes to a lot of other places."

"Still, it's interesting, don't you think? It also means that Darren isn't around Oxford to harass you or Gemma. Feel better now?"

I'd feel better when I saw Gemma myself. I'd feel even better when she opened her eyes and proved to all of us that she wasn't brain-damaged. But, for now, knowing she was being safely watched definitely helped. There was a certain irony in placing two vampires at the bedside of a beautiful young woman who might be dying anyway, but I had grown to trust my vampire knitting club and I knew that Mabel and Clara would protect her with everything they had. So I nodded. "I feel better."

Rafe said, "Professor Sanderson is giving a lecture tomorrow night. I think we should go. After the lecture we'll have a little chat with the professor."

He was obviously out of touch with Oxford events. I passed the Weston often and I'd seen the poster advertising the lecture countless times. "That lecture has been sold out for months."

He looked at me as though I was being incredibly naïve. "I have a certain amount of influence at the Bodleian. I don't think it will be difficult to acquire two tickets."

I may have bobbed my head and mimicked him in a rude voice reminiscent of Hester, the eternal whiny teenager, but inside I was pretty pleased with him. I tended to forget that, in his professional capacity, Rafe was an important person at the Bodleian.

"Do you think we'll be able to get close to him?" I imagined the elusive author might be mobbed after giving such a rare public lecture.

"There's a cocktail party afterwards, VIPs only, in the Old Bodleian across the street. We'll find time to talk to him." The way he said it made a shiver run down my spine. I got the feeling that if Rafe decided a person was going to talk to him, that person was going to be singing like a canary whether they wanted to or not.

CHAPTER 14

*T*he lecture was held in the Sheldonian Theatre and the gracious, Christopher Wren-designed dome was packed with people waiting to hear Dominic Sanderson. I glanced around and saw fans of all ages, more men than women but not by a huge margin. They were young and old of assorted nationalities and many had copies of the books with them. Some looked to be old treasured volumes that were well read, some were in foreign languages, and quite a few with the brand-new ones that had been reissued to celebrate the fortieth anniversary.

There was a buzz of anticipation as we waited. Dominic Sanderson was like a rock star of literature. I saw Professor Jeffrey Naylor in a tier above us. Rafe, of course, had perfect seats. We were directly across from the podium on the main level.

When Dominic Sanderson walked onto the stage accompanied by the man I recognized as his agent, the room broke into spontaneous applause. Sanderson looked like a scholar. He was tall and thin and tweedy. He had pair of reading glasses tucked into his pocket and a copy of the new edition of the Chronicles of Pangnirtung in his hand. No doubt a public relations exercise, as there were media photographers in the room. Any photographs taken would feature the new edition his publisher was trying to sell.

I was surprised at my own antagonism towards him. The tall, tweedy fake. I felt in my bones that he was not to be trusted. Even from this distance I was certain I detected something shifty in his eyes.

He and the agent sat together and chatted quietly for a few minutes and then Charles Beach, the agent, stood and approached the microphone. Rafe leaned close to me and said, "He's as much his personal promoter as his agent."

Charles Beach was about the same age as Sanderson, but was in every other way his polar opposite. Where Sanderson was tall he was on the short side. He was also plump, whereas Sanderson looked like the sort of person who would forget to eat because he was so caught up in his books.

The agent wore a blue striped suit and a yellow bow tie. He had a booming voice, so he really didn't need the mic. "Welcome." He waited for the shuffling and whispering to end and when the room was silent, he said, "My name is Charles Beach. I'm Chaz to my friends, and I'm proud and honored to call our guest this evening, Dominic Sanderson, one of those friends. When he first came to me in London, forty-one years ago, he'd just finished his undergraduate degree at Oxford. I'd only been a literary agent for a couple of years. We were both at the beginning of our careers.

"Dominic's novel had already been turned down by several publishers. This is not unusual in my business. However, I could see right away that there was something raw and powerful and exciting in his prose." He paused for the spontaneous clapping that erupted from the fans. I did the polite fake clap, where my hands moved but my palms didn't touch. I thought Rafe was doing the same.

He nodded and went on. "Dominic and I took a chance on each other. He, with an unproven agent, and me with an untried author." He turned and grinned back at his client. "It was a gamble that paid off handsomely for both of us."

Pause for more spontaneous applause.

"Many fantasy novels come and go. In the last four decades we've seen plenty. There aren't many that stick, that become part of the contemporary consciousness. The Chronicles of Pangnirtung is a series that will live forever."

I wondered how he could possibly know that, but the fans applauding madly obviously believed he could see into the future.

"I look around this wonderful theater and know that each of you have your own reasons for being here. Your own reasons for appreciating this man's genius. I don't need to tell you all of Dominic Sanderson's many accomplishments. He's a professor here at Oxford, at Cardinal College, because he loves to give back. He loves teaching and he loves his students. His books have hit every bestseller milestone and won many awards, and the success of the films has created an entire new generation of Chronicles of Pangnirtung fans." He waved his hand theatrically around the room. "Of whom you are but a small number. But a very special number. Please let me turn over the podium to my friend, Dominic Sanderson."

The clapping was thunderous. I tapped my hands together with more politeness than enthusiasm as Sanderson approached the podium and cleared his throat. He said,

"Thank you, Chaz. And thank you all for coming tonight." He had a dry voice. And took frequent sips of water as he spoke. But, he was an academic and a teacher, and he talked about the books and their symbolism as though he were teaching a class about them.

He told a couple of witty anecdotes, but he didn't strike me as a naturally humorous man. After about half an hour, he read a passage from one of the books. And then he stood to the side and Charles Beach returned to stand aside him. Now each of them had a microphone.

Charles said, "As you know, we took questions in advance. I will be asking the questions we received most commonly and Dominic will answer them. If there's time at the end, we will open the floor."

Rafe leaned in. "Interesting that they've already vetted the questions. They're playing it safe."

Charles, my-friends-call-me-Chaz, pulled out a piece of paper and turned to Dominic. "First question—and if I had a pound or a dollar for every time we get asked this question, I'd be a wealthy man, or I should say, a wealthier man. And Dominic would be a much wealthier man." He raised his hands in dramatic fashion. "When are you going to write another book?"

I was interested in the answer. I felt Rafe stiffen slightly at my side. Dominic Sanderson smiled, a dry, secretive smile, and patted the reissued novel that sat on the podium. "The Chronicles of Pangnirtung were a work of passion. A young man's books. I can't say I'll never write another one, because, perhaps, one day I shall. However, there's a symmetry to these three books. A completeness to the Chronicles. I do not want to be a writer who turns out endless volumes for the sake of making money."

Chaz threw up his hands again. They were like a comedy duo, the clown and the straight man. "I'm all about making money. But I have to respect my friend Dominic here. He's a genuine artist."

He moved on to the next question. "Who is your favorite author?" And so it went on. After about ten minutes of this back and forth, there was no remaining time for any questions from the floor. Which, I suspected had been deliberately organized so that Dominic would not be blindsided by anything embarrassing.

Then it was over. If I'd hoped to grab a moment with the author, I'd have been sorely disappointed, as many people in attendance were, who'd rushed forward to have their precious books signed only to find Sanderson was gone.

Sanderson and his agent disappeared back through the door they had come in from. There was no mingling, no book signing. Only the lucky ones who had tickets to the VIP reception would be rubbing shoulders with the famous author. I'd never been so grateful to have Rafe in my life.

It was a short walk across the street to the Bodleian. The cocktail party was held in the cavernous entrance hall, a massive space with high stone ceilings. Those who'd managed to get tickets for this event clustered in corners talking amongst themselves, but it was pretty obvious all eyes were on the door, waiting for the guest of honor to arrive. Rafe collected two glasses of red wine for us from a long table where Bodleian staff members were serving. There were also appetizers going around on trays. I shook my head as one went by. I was too nervous to eat.

I said to Rafe, in a low voice, "What's our plan? What do we do when we finally get Dominic Sanderson to ourselves?"

"I wonder if you should stick to the story you made up for Jeffrey Naylor yesterday. You're an American grad student, and you're interested in his background and influences."

I felt panicked at the very idea. "What if he asks me what my favorite scene is? Or tests me in some way? He'll know right away I'm lying."

He looked at me and shook his head. "You really never read the Chronicles?"

"No. I really never have. I read Jane Austen and novels about female empowerment."

"Perhaps you should talk to the agent, then. He'll be easier to get to anyway. Everyone here wants a few words with Dominic Sanderson, but few will be interested in the agent."

I liked that plan much better. Charles Beach looked exactly like the sort of man who was more interested in hearing his own voice than in listening. Exactly the kind I wanted. "But what do I ask him?"

"Stick to the same story. You're looking for influences. Ask him about that first meeting, and casually bring up the scandal. You could pretend you've only just discovered it as part of your research and you want his take on it."

"You'd better be ready to rescue me if I flounder."

"Buck up. You won't flounder." And then he raised a hand in greeting and a well-dressed older couple came over and greeted him by name. Rafe said, "Lord and Lady Mead, may I present Lucy Swift. I did some work for them last year."

They both shook my hand. Lady Mead smiled at me. "It was very exciting. Rafe looked through our collection of books, some of which had been sitting on the shelves for hundreds of years, probably never even opened, and discovered we had a rare first edition of Gulliver's Travels. Imagine!"

Rafe said, "It was an exciting day for me, too. There aren't many of those left in the world. It's always gratifying to discover a treasure."

A sudden buzz of excitement went around the room, and I knew that Dominic Sanderson must've arrived. Sure enough, we all turned and there he was walking in with his agent.

Lord Mead said, "Of course, we've got first editions of the Chronicles, too. I read all the books when they first came out. Astonishing. I just purchased the new set for my grandson. He's only ten, but I was able to get Professor Sanderson to sign them. It's going to be his Christmas gift."

His wife looked at him fondly. "My husband is more excited, I'm sure, than our grandson will be."

"You don't know that. He's a very bright young man."

They excused themselves to try and get a few words with Dominic Sanderson. Rafe and I watched as a crowd formed around the author, but luck was with us, when the agent headed towards the drinks table.

I took a quick breath and said, "Wish me luck." I grabbed Rafe's glass and poured the rest of my red wine into it and then carried my empty glass over toward the table where wine and water were being served. I managed to arrive exactly when the agent did. He helped himself to a glass of red and I did the same.

I said, "I enjoyed that talk so much."

He gave me the professionally pleasant look that speakers give to strangers. "Glad you enjoyed it."

Before he could move away, I said, "I'm so pleased to have

a chance to speak with you. My name is Lucy Swift, I'm a grad student from Boston. I'm here doing my thesis on Dr. Sanderson's novels."

His smile deepened, but only slightly. "Excellent timing, with the fortieth anniversary celebrations."

"Exactly." I said, looking enthusiastic. "I'm most interested in the very beginning of Dominic Sanderson's career. Tell me what it was like for you, when he walked into your office, when you first read his work."

He glanced over to make sure Dominic Sanderson was well entertained, which he was. "It was electrifying. As you know, when you first dive into those novels, they take you into a completely different world. So much fantasy, I'm sorry to say, is derivative. But this was so fresh and bold. I suppose, because I was just starting out, I could give the manuscript all of my attention and all of my energy." He smirked a little here. "And I had a lot more energy forty years ago." He shrugged. "Also I was hungrier. I was willing to work as hard as Sanderson was to make those books succeed."

"I'm studying his early influences, particularly his friendship with another student, one that went badly wrong."

The expression of patronizing bonhomie disappeared and suddenly Charles Beach's eyes went hard. "That was devastating for Dominic. Absolutely devastating. His old friend stealing his ideas and laying claim to his work like that. I wouldn't be a bit surprised if that's why he was never able to write another book. It broke his heart."

"But, as his agent, weren't you even a little bit worried that the story might be true? I imagine it would have damaged your career as much as it would have Dominic Sanderson's if the books had turned out to be written by someone else."

He looked a much less pleasant man now. He said, "The man was a drunk and raving mad." He shook his head. "He caused Dominic anguish just when he should have been enjoying his success."

He glanced back at Sanderson, still surrounded by a small crowd. "I promised I'd get Dominic a drink. He'll be so mobbed all evening, he'll never get a chance to get his own."

I smiled. "Of course. I'm so glad I got a chance to speak with you."

He grabbed a second glass of wine and said, "Don't waste your time on that filthy old scandal. If you really want to delve into Dominic Sanderson's early influences, call my office. We'll set up an appointment. I may even be able to get you a few minutes with the man himself. But run your questions by me first."

"Of course." He handed me a business card and I took it eagerly. "I can't tell you how grateful I am," I gushed. But inside my stomach was churning. Martin Hodgins was on a slab in a morgue right now, while Sanderson sipped wine and accepted accolades for work that wasn't his. Somehow, I was going to see that justice was done, for his reputation and for Gemma.

Charles Beach turned, with the two glasses of wine in his hands. "Dominic wouldn't be here without his fans, and he always tries to give back."

I was hoping he'd have a chance to really give back. He could give the stolen manuscript back to its rightful owner, who, I supposed, was now Gemma.

Rafe was chatting to an intense young woman who listened to him so eagerly she was practically licking up his words. I was surprised at the shaft of discomfort I felt. If he were a different kind of man, I'd have thought it was jealousy. But there were things about Rafe that made him a very unsuitable partner, like the whole undead thing. Still, he was an extremely attractive man. And she clearly thought so.

I left him to it and wandered around the room reviewing my brief conversation with Charles Beach. I wondered if I would take him up on his offer. I could get Rafe to help me come up with some innocuous sounding questions and then, when I actually had a one-on-one interview with Dominic Sanderson, I could ask the questions I really wanted answered.

"Well, hello. Fancy seeing you here." I glanced up to see Ian Chisholm walking up to me with a smile on his face. I returned it. "You got a night off. Congratulations."

"I was determined to come. Bought the ticket months ago. What are you doing here? Haven't suddenly turned into a Sanderson fan, have you?"

"No. Rafe Crosyer had two tickets. He invited me. But, I was just thinking I should read the Chronicles. I've never been a fantasy reader, but they do sound fascinating."

"They are. I think you'll enjoy them."

"Did you get a chance to chat to Dominic Sanderson?" I asked him.

He gazed across the room. "Not a hope. I hovered at the edge of the crowd around him for couple of minutes, but he's got a soft voice, I couldn't really hear what he was saying. I gave up in the end. Maybe I'll get a moment later to tell him how much the books meant to me. Still, at least I got him to sign the new edition. That was something."

I glanced around and when I was certain there was no

one close enough to hear us, I asked, "Were you able to reach Gemma's father?"

He scratched his head. And I thought he looked disappointed to be talking about police business when he was actually enjoying a social night out. "The father seems to be a bit of a recluse. He has no phone. No email. Local police paid him a visit yesterday morning, I believe and told him about his daughter." He looked as though he might say more and then stopped himself. I suspected he'd already heard about the fire.

"Did you hear the news?"

Maybe he was going to tell me about the fire, except that he sounded as though he had good news. I shook my head. He said, "Gemma squeezed her grandmother's hand."

I knew very well that the hand she squeezed wasn't her grandmother's. But still, it seemed a very exciting development. I felt a smile bloom. "When did it happen? That's good news, right? What did the doctor say?"

He held up a hand and laughed. "Whoa. It happened earlier this evening. I checked messages between the lecture and coming over here. That's when I heard. The doctors definitely think it's a good sign. They won't commit themselves further than that."

I decided that it was an excellent sign. He glanced behind me and then said, "Well, let me know how you get on with the books. Once you're done, perhaps we can discuss them." He leaned in and dropped his voice. "The crowd around Sanderson looks a little lighter. Think I'll have another go."

I wished him luck and he walked off. Almost immediately, Rafe come up to my side. "Detective Inspector Chisholm is quite a fan."

I glanced at him sharply, because it sounded to me that it wasn't Dominic Sanderson he was referring to as the object of Ian's interest. He was one to talk, with that intense young woman who'd practically been drooling on him.

"How was your conversation with the agent?"

"Very interesting." I showed him the business card. And then related the conversation as well as I could remember it.

Rafe rolled his eyes. "So he deflected your questions and insisted that you'd get no help for your thesis unless you followed a line of inquiry more flattering to his client."

"Exactly. But here's the interesting thing. He had instant recall of the name, when the scandal was forty years ago."

"The name's fresh in his mind."

"Dominic Sanderson's got a lot more money and clout now, than when he was in his twenties." I gazed across at the author, still surrounded by eagerly chatting fans. "Maybe Martin Hodgins didn't just send a piece of that manuscript to his daughter. Maybe he also sent a section to Dominic Sanderson."

"And Sanderson decided to get rid of his old friend permanently."

I could picture the whole scene. "It would be so easy. He phones up his old friend. Says, Hodge, old buddy, I got your manuscript. Let's bury the hatchet. Why don't I drop by your house and we'll talk about this. Have a drink for old times. Maybe I don't want to give up my reputation or my name on this book, but I'd be happy to make a sizeable financial contribution to your retirement."

Rafe nodded. He was also watching Sanderson, so at home with the adulation and the fans. "So he goes to see his old friend. He probably takes a bottle of scotch or whatever his drink of choice is these days. He takes a few sips to be polite and presses more and more drink on Martin Hodgins."

I picked up the thread again. It was playing like a movie in my head. "Maybe Sanderson *was* prepared to pay up. But Hodgins doesn't want money. Not anymore. He probably never did. Everyone says those books are full of passion. They were his life's work. His greatest achievement. He wants the credit. He wants his name on those books. Sanderson can't have that. So, he gets Martin Hodgins so drunk he passes out." I looked at Rafe. "And then what? He lights a cigarette and starts the fire? How could he possibly know that would be enough to kill the man?"

"More likely he made sure he was dead before the fire started." He shook his head. "Smothered him to death with a pillow, maybe? If he was smart, he made sure Hodgins breathed in a few lungfuls of smoke first, so smoke inhalation would show up in the post mortem. It's cold-blooded, but quite a brilliant way to get rid of an adversary. No one would ever know he committed murder."

I took a sip of wine, hoping it would ease my aching throat. Just thinking about smoke inhalation and suffocation made my throat hurt. "Imagine having to live with that all your life. First, knowing that everything you were famous for was a lie. And then, taking a former friend's life in order to perpetuate that lie." I shook my head. "How does a man like that live with himself?"

Rafe and I were still watching the author, glad-handing and chuckling, signing books that were shoved under his nose. Rafe said, "He doesn't look like he's having much trouble living with himself. He's probably created his own fiction around the success. Talked himself into believing that those novels were half his anyway because he'd talked them over so often with Martin Hodgins. And, if Martin had been reasonable, they could've made an arrangement. In his mind, Martin probably caused his own death, by being obstinate."

I couldn't even look at the author anymore. "I guess you've had more experience of evil people than I have."

He nodded, grimly. "In six centuries of dealing with humanity, that is undoubtedly true."

I put down my glass. "Well, even free wine and hanging out with lords and ladies isn't enough to keep me here another minute."

We walked out into the cold night air. Rafe turned to me. "Well? Can I buy you a glass of wine that I can assure you will be of a higher quality?"

I had to laugh. "Have you always been this much of a snob?"

"I'd say that life is too short to drink bad wine. But, in my case, that's clearly not true."

I was shocked. "Rafe Crosyer, did you just make a joke?"

He looked down his snooty nose at me. "I'm not devoid of humor."

I let that go. "What I really want to do is go back to my place and see how Clara and Mabel made out with Gemma today. Ian told me that Gemma squeezed the hand of which-ever one is pretending to be her grandmother." I looked at him uncertainly. "That's good news, right?"

"I'm no doctor, but I should think so."

CHAPTER 15

*W*e got back to my flat and found the knitting club was working at its usual, ferocious pace. I noticed that every time Christopher Weaver showed up, he set the bar a little higher. He had now begun to inset pieces of embroidery into his stockings. They were exquisite scenes that were works of art on their own. Naturally, the vampires were now embroidering, as well as knitting, equally quickly.

Nyx had discovered the Christmas stockings were just the right size for her. She had somehow crawled into one of them and was peacefully asleep, her black head and one paw emerging from the top of one of the stockings laying on top of the table, looking like the most adorable Christmas gift ever.

After I'd gushed over everyone's work, which was easy to do as all their work was amazing, I asked Clara, who was present, about the news from hospital.

Her sweet face was suffused with smiles. "She squeezed my hand." She glanced around at the group. "It's true. I didn't want to say anything until Lucy got here, but dear, sweet, Gemma squeezed my hand today."

"But you're not even her real grandmother."

"And I don't pretend to be. We told a bit of a porky pie to the medical people in order to be able to help your friend, but I wouldn't demean myself to lie to a young woman in a coma. It wouldn't be right."

"What do pork pies have to do with anything," I asked, feeling extremely confused.

Theodore chuckled. "Porky pie is Cockney rhyming slang for a lie."

Sometimes, I really understood how Meri felt, confused by the customs of a completely foreign society. Porky pies. Honestly. "So, how did she come to squeeze your hand?"

"I talked a lot about you, Lucy, because you and she were friends. I was talking about your knitting, and how you're getting better all the time." She patted my hand. "You are, you know. One day, you will be as proficient with the needles as your grandmother."

Unless I became undead and had hundreds of years to practice, I very much doubted that would happen. And, since I had no intention of turning into a vampire, I was going to have to accept that at knitting, at least, I sucked. However, I didn't say that. I said, "Do you remember your exact words?"

She paused in her knitting and gazed up at the ceiling. "I think I said, Lucy is getting so much better at her knitting. And when she comes to see you next, I'll encourage her to bring hers along. It's very soothing to have your knitting by you when you're sitting in the hospital for long hours." She shook her head. "If Mabel were here, she could probably give it to you word for word, but that was the gist of it. I was just talking."

Had Gemma just randomly chosen to squeeze Clara's

hand? Or, even from that dark place where she currently was, was she trying to get a message across? Perhaps she was trying to warn me not to visit her. Because she thought she was still in danger.

"And Mabel's there now?"

"Oh, yes. We won't leave her. One of us is always there." She hesitated. "Alfred told us about the fire. Poor Gemma. I almost dread her waking up, knowing she must find out she's lost her other parent. It reminds me of the Blitz, you know. In the war, everyone lost people they loved. Terrible, it was."

This wasn't war, though, it was murder. I wanted to rush to the hospital and sit beside Gemma all night, but I knew that was foolish. Mabel was accustomed to staying up all night. It was her natural waking time. I'd be no good to anyone if I deprived myself of sleep. I was tired as it was.

"I'll go and visit her tomorrow."

"You will be careful, won't you? Someone very dangerous is out there. Gemma didn't put herself in that coma."

No, she hadn't. The question was, who had? And how are we going to catch them?

I SLEPT DEEPLY AND WELL. Somehow knowing there was an entire nest of vampires just downstairs made me feel safe. Rafe had settled down to join them and it added to my sense of safety knowing he'd be down there all night.

Meri and I went down to the shop together in the morning. I needed to put in another huge wool order to keep up with the Christmas stocking factory. With only a week left of the holiday market, we were expecting even bigger crowds.

There was also extra work in Cardinal Woolsey's. I was glad to have two assistants out front as that gave me time to get to work packing shipments.

I was working in the back, packing up the mail-orders, some of which were Christmas gifts that I wanted to make sure arrived in plenty of time. It was peaceful work and allowed my mind free rein. Not that they were particularly happy thoughts galloping around in my head. I was think about Gemma, and her poor father, and Dominic Sanderson, and Darren the stalker.

I hated that Gemma's attacker and, presumably, her father's murderer, was out there. Gemma would never be safe until he was caught. But how were we to do that?

Meanwhile, the cheerful bells kept announcing new customers in the shop. Meri and Violet between them seemed perfectly able to take care of the customers. It was nice working in the back quietly by myself, hearing the cheerful chatter and the very satisfying sound of the cash register ringing up another purchase.

I was no closer to an answer of how to trap Gemma's attacker, when I heard a voice out front that I thought was Ian's. I paused in the middle of taping my latest package shut when I heard him say, "Is Lucy around?"

I was mildly flattered. Violet said, in her clear voice, "Lucy? There's someone to see you."

I called out. "You can come on back."

Ian pulled the curtain back and stepped in to my back room. Any idea I'd had that he was here on a social visit swiftly vanished when I saw the look on his face. Thunderous was the word that best described his expression.

I raised my brows. "Ian. What brings you here?"

"I don't know where to start." He paced rapidly back-and-forth. It wasn't a very big room so it didn't take him long. "Gemma Hodgins' hotel room was broken into."

My eyes widened. "What?"

He shook her finger at me. "Don't you play the innocent with me, Lucy Swift. We went over the CCTV footage. What were you doing there? And don't even pretend to tell me you were visiting Gemma because at the time that footage was taken she was already in hospital."

His anger was firing mine. "Are you accusing me of breaking into her room?" I thought going on the attack was my best form of defense. I hadn't actually broken into her room, I'd magicked my way in. There was a difference. And I certainly hadn't damaged anything. There was no way the police could have suspected a break-in based on Rafe's and my visit, which made me certain someone else had done the breaking and entering.

He looked as though he didn't know what he believed. "Don't play games with me. What were you doing there?"

I was thinking rapidly. I was positive there hadn't been any cameras in the hotel hallways. They could only have been in the lobby and outdoors. At most the cameras had picked me up going in and possibly walking out with a package, though, when I came to think of it, Rafe and I'd slipped out the back way. I said, "I'd had a package dropped off for her. It was one of our Christmas stockings. I just thought it would cheer up her room. But, after she was in hospital, it seemed stupid and depressing to have a Christmas decoration waiting for her when she returned. So, I went to pick it up again."

His eyes narrowed on my face. "And that's all you did?"

I put my hands on my hips. I was still holding the tape dispenser so I whacked myself a good one. "Just what, exactly, are you accusing me of?"

"Someone turned her room upside down. They were obviously looking for something. Do you know what that could've been?"

"No." I stepped forward and got right into his face. "Do you know why someone tried to murder her?" Which seemed to me a more relevant question.

His face grew ruddy. "That is what I am trying to find out." He said each word separately and very deliberately.

He paced across my room and back again once more. "Gemma's father's house burned to the ground the day before yesterday. I suppose you don't know anything about that, either?"

"Why would I?"

He turned on me. "Because, a uniformed officer at the scene said a black Tesla drew up with a man and a woman inside. They said they were there to visit the occupant of the house that had just burned to the ground. He described the people in the car. One of them sounded very much like you. And the other sounded like a certain antiquarian book expert who owns a black Tesla."

Busted.

I put the tape dispenser down on the table beside the stack of neatly wrapped packages. "Okay. I asked Rafe to drive me to Gemma's father's house. I wanted to encourage him to visit her. We were going to offer to drive him back to Oxford with us."

"You know they retrieved a body?"

I closed my eyes. But like a film playing on the back of my

eyelids, I saw that sad lump on the stretcher being wheeled and put into the back of the ambulance. I nodded.

"What is it about you, Lucy?" The words seemed to explode out of him. "Where you go, disaster follows."

"That is so unfair. By the time I got there, the house had already burned down. I had nothing to do with it."

"What do you know? What aren't you telling me?"

I was as irritated and frustrated as he was. "I tried to tell you about Darren, the ex-boyfriend, and you weren't interested. Did you know that Darren left town on his motorcycle the night before the fire?"

I could tell from his expression that he didn't know that. Because, obviously, they weren't watching Darren's movements. He narrowed his eyes. "Go on."

"Did you know that Gemma's father and Dominic Sanderson were best mates at school? Here at Oxford. Gemma's father claimed to be the true author of the Chronicles of Pangnirtung "

Understanding dawned in his green eyes. "Hodgins." He nodded. "Martin Hodgins. That's why the name was vaguely familiar. I'd read about the scandal somewhere. So, Gemma Hodgins is his daughter." He looked at me, puzzled. "You don't seriously believe Martin Hodgins was the true author, do you? He was completely discredited at the time. He's in the Wikipedia entry as a footnote. Or a joke."

"What if it's not a joke?"

He shook his head. "Do you have any proof of this at all?"

I couldn't tell him about the manuscript we'd liberated from her hotel room. "No, I don't have any proof. But it's interesting, don't you think? That Gemma was attacked and her father murdered within a week of each other?"

"We don't have confirmation on the identity of the corpse yet."

I made a rude noise. "Who else could it be?"

"All right. It's probably Martin Hodgins. But, unlike you, I don't go haring off making assumptions. He pointed his finger at me. "I deal in proof and evidence."

I deal in magic and mayhem.

"That's why you were there, last night, wasn't it? Because of these wild suspicions of yours. I suppose Gemma put the idea in your head that her father was the real author of the Chronicles of Pangnirtung."

"As a matter of fact, she did. Of course, she's a loving daughter. But, what if she's right?" It was my turn to jab my finger towards his face. "I think a man who had as much at stake as Dominic Sanderson does might go to great lengths to keep his fame and riches and his reputation. What do you think?"

"I think you should leave the policing to the professionals." He glanced at the packages I was wrapping. "And stick to your knitting."

Before I could come up with a sufficiently annihilating response, he'd stomped out of my back room. A minute later I heard the bells chime as he went back out the front door. They no longer sounded like happy bells.

CHAPTER 16

J was too annoyed to wrap any more packages. I decided to stretch my legs and walk the ones I'd done down to the post office. First, I took a few minutes for myself, pacing back and forth until the tingly feeling in my fingertips had eased. The last thing I needed was to be walking down Harrington Street or, even worse, hectic Cornmarket Street, and have all the packages in my arms go up in flames by spontaneous combustion.

By the time I was sufficiently in control of myself to go back out front, my arms full of packages, Meri and Violet both stared at me with wide eyes. Violet said, "I never knew you had such a temper."

"Of course you did. I remember how mad I was at you when we first met."

She tipped her head in acknowledgement. "All right. I didn't know you had such a temper where the dishy inspector was concerned."

"Ha. If you think he's so dishy why don't you take him off my hands?"

She tossed her hair, and the pink stripe dyed down the front of her black hair shook like a birthday party ribbon. "I would, but he doesn't seem to have eyes for anyone but you."

For some reason this irritated me even more. I grabbed the biggest carry bag I could find and shoved packages into it. "I'm going to the post office and then I may go for a long walk. If anyone needs me you can ring me on my mobile."

A brisk walk to the post office helped clear my head and cool my irritation. I was given printed pages containing tracking numbers so I could make sure all the parcels got to where they were going. There was real satisfaction in mailing off all these packages to people around the world who relied on my knitting shop.

I wasn't in a hurry to get back, and Violet and Meri were clearly well able to take care of the shop without me. I walked up to the University Parks, which was a good place to think. Even in the cold weather there were a surprising number of joggers, and people walking dogs and pushing strollers. Students holding hands. I chewed over what Ian had said. That someone had broken into Gemma's hotel room. She'd had no valuables. I didn't believe for a moment that someone was so passionately interested in her soap and bath bombs they'd broken in to get them for free. The only thing worth stealing was that manuscript.

But, was I jumping to conclusions? Just because Rafe and I had found value in the manuscript didn't mean that whoever had broken in felt the same way. Could it have been Darren? In his rage, had he broken into Gemma's room?

I wished now, that instead of yelling back at Ian, I had probed a little more about exactly what had been done to her hotel room. The crazed ex would act differently than someone searching for hidden treasure, in this case a chunk of manuscript.

So who'd been in her room, and why?

As I walked past a young couple who were steaming up the cold day, getting very intimate on a park bench, I was determined to find out.

I walked along the bank of the river Cherwell. It was too cold for the punters who plied the flat boats up and down in the warmer weather. It was almost too cold for the ducks and geese. They huddled together, looking as though they wished they'd flown south when they had the chance. I didn't blame them. At least I had somewhere warmer to go and I decided to head back. A man jogged past me in tiny shorts and a singlet, his skinny white arms pumping back-and-forth. He streamed sweat and I basked for a moment in the cloud of warmth as he sprinted past.

I passed through the gate and pushed the button for the crosswalk light. Traffic was sparse but, with the left and right thing, I hesitated to jaywalk. I was waiting patiently, my thoughts far away, when the rumble of a motorcycle, that I'd vaguely noted, grew louder. I glanced to my left and, in horror, saw a bike bearing down on me.

It was headed straight for me. I leapt back, and the wheels came up onto the indentation where the sidewalk ramps down, level to the road. I screamed and threw myself backward, stumbling and falling hard on my butt. I scrambled back and he missed my toes by an inch and then the engine screamed as he roared off again, not racing away, but turning the bike to have another go at me. I was sprayed by bits of gravel and muddy water and as the bike turned I saw the green decal of a rocket ship. The words Fuel Rocket had been amended by a Sharpie pen so they read Babe Magnet. I did not think many people vandalized their own stickers that way. It was Darren.

I was frozen for a second, sitting on the cold ground frantically trying to think of the right spell. Make me disappear? Make him disappear? Protection spell. Protection spell. *Think!*

The bike turned and started toward me. The black helmet seemed particularly sinister with the visor pulled down. My words stumbled and started and my voice shook, but words appeared in my head as though someone else had put them there. I swear I smelled tuna, which reminded me of Nyx and how I wished my familiar was here.

The words didn't make much sense to me. I decided then and there that if I survived I was going to learn Latin. I recognized the word *vitreus*, which I thought meant glass. And I thought *protego* must mean protect. For the rest, I just read them out loud without any idea of their meaning. I believed in magic, but I didn't always believe in my own talent with it. For all I knew, I'd just fixed somebody's window. I scrambled to my feet and started to run. I'd dropped my carry bag with the tracking numbers in it but I couldn't worry about that.

As I ran, I heard the engine roar, coming closer, and then the most satisfying sound. Like a rock hitting a windshield.

Bang.

I turned my head over my shoulder and saw bike and man fall to the ground. But I wasn't stupid enough to go near that psychopath killer. I kept running.

When I was certain he wasn't chasing me, I ducked behind the wall of a red brick apartment complex, pulled my mobile phone out with shaking hands and hit Ian's number.

"Detective inspector Chisholm," he said, as though he didn't know perfectly well who was calling.

"I want to report a hit-and-run." My voice came out high and far too hysterical for my liking. I swallowed. *Get a grip.*

"What?"

Then, I realized I was about to make fool of myself, so I amended my complaint to, "Attempted hit-and-run."

"Lucy? What happened?"

I told him, succinctly, exactly what had happened. "Darren is a menace and a dangerous one. How much evidence do you need before you arrest him?"

"Is he there now?"

"Would I be standing here talking to you if a murderer was beside me? No! I'm pretty sure I heard him ride away. I'm hiding behind the wall of an apartment complex."

"Good. Do you want me to come and get you?"

Now that I wasn't dead and the intensity of my adrenalin flow was less like Niagara Falls and more like a dripping tap, I was calmer. The last thing I wanted was the police rushing to my side. "No. I'm going back to the shop. I'm not hurt." Though I was pretty sure my butt and hip were going to bloom with bruises. They were already sore.

"Take me through it, again. Take a deep breath first. Slow down. And tell me exactly what happened."

I was so angry I was shaking. Reaction was setting in. I didn't know if Darren had actually intended to kill me, but I did not think that encounter would have ended well for me if not for the magic spell. It had seriously been magic the way the words had appeared in my mind like a teleprompter was installed in my brain.

He muttered something that I think included a curse

word or two. "I'll have him brought in for questioning. I'll need you to come in and make a statement, though."

Why did the victim always end up with extra work? It seemed so unfair. However, I understood he was only doing his job, so I agreed. I'd been in a bad mood when I started my walk, and, by the time I limped into the shop, I was in a worse one.

Violet looked up anxiously, the minute I walked in the door. "Oh, Lucy, thank goddess."

I was surprised at her vehemence, and then Nyx all but launched herself into my arms and snuggled against me, purring madly. I could feel her heartbeat frantic against my palm. I buried my face in her fur. "It's all right, Nyx. It's all right." I smelled tuna and recalled smelling that same tuna-breath smell when the exact spell I'd needed had appeared in my head. "Thanks, pal," I whispered.

"Whatever's been happening?" Violet raised her voice. "Nyx was like a caged lion. And, I mean, exactly like a caged lion. Walking back-and-forth, back-and-forth and meowing piteously in the front window. I was frightened to let her out in case she was having some kind of fit."

I glanced around but there was only one customer in the corner talking intently to Meri about a crochet pattern. I beckoned Violet over and explained, in a low voice, what had happened.

Like Ian, she asked, "Are you all right?"

I nodded. "I think so. I tripped on the sidewalk as I was trying to get away. I bruised my hip. Nothing a hot bath won't help." I'd just put the bag containing all the tracking numbers in the back. Then I realized the bag was gone. It must have fallen from my shoulder when I fell. I still had my small backpack, but the carry bag must be on the pavement where I'd fallen. I told Violet but she shook her head. "You're not going back there. I'll drive you later. Was there anything valuable in the bag?"

"No. But if someone doesn't get their package, I want to be able to track it."

"Lucy, you have more important things to worry about. Look at you!" Violet grabbed my hands and with a *brrrp*, Nyx crawled up and balanced on her belly, so she hung over my shoulder. It would have taken brute force to separate us. I knew Nyx had saved me. I think we both needed to stay connected for a while.

Violet said, "Oh, your lovely mittens are ruined. And you've scraped your hands."

I hadn't even noticed, but she was right. My bright red mitts were torn, and underneath my palms were streaked with dirt and a couple of scrapes were bleeding. Violet said, "Meri? Lucy and I are going upstairs for a few minutes. You'll be all right?"

Meri looked slightly harassed but one glance and I could tell she understood something bad had happened. "Of course. I shall be fine."

My hip protested as we climbed the stairs but Violet was right. I needed to clean the dirt off my hands, change my clothes and maybe there was some antibiotic ointment in the bathroom.

Because it was the middle of the day, there were no vampires in the upstairs flat. I'd have liked a hug and some fussing from my grandmother, but otherwise it was a relief not to have to answer a lot of questions.

Violet ushered me into the bathroom and insisted on

taking off my mittens herself. "They're ruined," she announced. "Such a shame."

A pair of ruined mittens was the least of my problems. She bathed my hands in water and soap and then patted them dry. Nyx made a sound of disgust, probably because it was so unmagical, and Violet said, "Be quiet, you. Naughty puss." To me, she said, "You don't need magic for everything."

That was a relief, since I was so bad at magic my cat had to send me spells by telepathy.

Violet helped me undress, which involved removing Nyx from my shoulder. She jumped to the bed and sat, staring at me, as though not trusting me out of her sight. Smart cat.

Once I was wrapped in my bathrobe and had fuzzy slippers on my feet, Violet took me out to the kitchen. I felt like a child being fussed over by her mother but I was really happy to have someone fussing over me. I felt shaken, bruised and stunned. Having a crazed killer after you in broad daylight will do that.

I sat down very slowly, wincing as my bottom settled painfully onto the chair. Nyx barely waited for me to stop wincing before jumping onto my lap. I didn't care if she made the pain worse, I needed my familiar right now. The way she was purring, I thought she felt the same way about me.

Violet put the kettle on and I thought, with some amusement, how very English that was. Nothing like a cup of tea to cure every ill from heartbreak to attempted murder. I said, "The tea's in the Queen Elizabeth's Royal Jubilee canister on that shelf there." I pointed to the bright blue can with the royal coat of arms, as though she could possibly miss it.

"You're having my special tea." Then, as I watched, she went into Gran's cupboards. At the back were the dried herbs she kept in packages, and some bottles of liquids I hadn't known what to do with. It seemed Violet did. She pulled out bags and bottles, muttered and shook her head. "Really, Lucy, you need to keep your pantry better stocked, and with fresher herbs."

I suspected she didn't have cooking in mind, so I kept my mouth shut and watched. She put bits of dried herb into a teapot, and added something that looked like old mushroom, or twigs, or maybe yak dung. She poured boiling water over the mess and waited a couple of minutes. Then she lifted the lid, inhaled the steam, shook her head and added more yak dung. After another minute, she repeated the lid-lifting, sniffing process and then, seeming satisfied, she found a tea strainer in the cutlery drawer and a large china mug commemorating the birth of Prince George. Into the royal mug she poured a brew that was the color of regular tea, but smelled like a stagnant bog.

She pushed the evil-looking concoction at me and nodded. "Drink up," she said briskly.

"You're not having any?" Not only was I thinking that misery loved company, but I wasn't entirely sure I trusted my witchy cousin. I'd feel happier if we both drank her stinky tea.

She raised her eyebrows. "I'm not wounded and bleeding. Come now, it will make you feel better."

Nyx was curled on my lap and since she wasn't hissing and spitting I decided to trust the tea. I took a sip and all my worst fears were confirmed. It tasted like a stagnant bog— that someone had peed in. My face screwed up in disgust. "This is revolting."

She shook her head at me. "You are such a baby." Then

she got up and fetched a pot of honey so old the liquid had crystalized. She pointed at it and gave an order in a language I didn't understand and the solidified honey obligingly melted to a gorgeous, golden liquid. I dropped in a large spoonful into my mug and stirred it around. It didn't make the brew taste good, but at least I could choke it down, stopping at regular intervals to gag and moan.

"Drink your tea," she insisted when I'd stopped to gasp.

"Calling that muck tea is an insult to tea everywhere."

"You're stalling, Lucy. Drink it while it's hot."

When I'd got about halfway through the drink, I realized that my hip wasn't hurting anymore. I shifted experimentally and to my surprise, my aches were all but gone.

I opened my hands and saw that the bleeding had stopped, though the skin was still broken and smarting. Nyx raised her head and licked my palm. Her sandpaper tongue smarted but even as I pulled my hand away, I saw that the scrapes were closing.

I offered her my other palm and she obligingly cat-kissed it all better.

After that, I stopped complaining and finished my tea. My fellow witches, both human and animal, looked pleased when I was done. Violet said, "I'll leave you the recipe for that. In fact, I've got a few indispensible potions you should have. Love potion, obviously, a calming tea, one that helps ease pregnancy aches, and, of course, the healing potion you've just drunk."

We hadn't always been the best of friends, but I felt we were both reaching for a tentative friendship. I suspected she'd always be competitive, but she'd also been there when I'd needed her. I wouldn't forget that.

In between forcing down the evil-tasting potion, I'd shared all the details of the motorcycle attack. I left out the bit where Nyx had passed me the spell. Maybe I was a little competitive too, where Violet was concerned. Let her think I was getting on with our family grimoire and actually learning the spells. When I'd finished my recital, she said, "I'm very glad you're pressing charges. He nearly killed Gemma. We know what he's capable of."

And then she patted Nyx on the head. "And you've got a very loyal familiar, there. I believe, if you hadn't arrived home soon, she'd have cast her own spell to go and find you."

Nyx looked up at me and I winked at her.

Sometimes I felt very much alone in Oxford. But not when I had a purring familiar in my arms, a concerned cousin, and a detective inspector who was trying his level best to keep me out of harm's way.

My bad mood began to abate.

Violet said, "Why don't I drive you down to Kidlington when you're ready to give your statement."

"You don't have to do that. I have a car."

She shook her head. "I've seen you drive. And you've had a shock. I didn't heal you to send you off to a traffic accident. I'll drive you."

Since she was right, I was having trouble getting the hang of driving on the left, I agreed.

She went back downstairs to the shop and I took a quick shower, then dressed in a royal blue extra long sweater that Alfred had knitted me. He said he chose the color of the wool to match my eyes. It was one of those garments that just made me happy, and I needed the comfort. Wearing it was like wrapping myself in a hug from someone who cared about me.

I wore wool stockings underneath and, instead of my boots, I chose black running shoes. Maybe I was shutting the barn door after the horse had already bolted, but I wanted to be able to run next time a crazed motorcycle riding killer came at me.

I like to be prepared like that.

I freshened my makeup, not because I was seeing Ian later, but because I liked to look nice for my customers.

When we closed for the day, the pair of us got into Violet's car, which was not much bigger than the car I'd inherited from Gran, but certainly newer. She drove it about twice the speed I normally drove, but she was a good driver and I relaxed next to her.

I had phoned ahead to let Ian know that we were on our way, and he was there to greet us. He looked me up and down as though making sure I didn't have any broken bones or bits missing. I said, "Did you catch him yet?"

He shook his head. He looked very grim. "But we will." Somehow his confidence made me believe that he would, indeed, catch Darren. The sooner that punk was off the streets the better.

To her obvious disappointment, Violet had to sit out in the waiting room. Ian took me into a conference room. He asked if it was all right to record our conversation and I said it was. Once more, I related exactly what had happened, leaving out the spell, obviously. I told him I'd heard a crash behind me and kept running, which was true. I just left out the bit where Nyx and I had caused the crash.

"Were you able to positively identify the motorcycle driver as Darren—Do we have his surname?"

What was he? Darren's lawyer? "Obviously it was him. He was riding Darren's bike."

"I do need you to be absolutely specific. Lots of motorbikes look similar. Did you see the rider's face?"

I opened my mouth and closed it again. Had I? The nightmare scene played in front of my eyes again. "He wore a black helmet with the visor down. But I recognized his black motorcycle."

"How? There are a lot of black motorcycles."

I reminded myself that he was doing his job, but I'd nearly been killed and I knew exactly who'd been behind that visor. Still, I did my best to keep my voice as calm and level as Ian's. "Darren's motorbike has a decal on it. But he'd written over the words Fuel Rocket with a black Sharpie. Now it says, Babe Magnet." The recorder couldn't catch my eye roll, which was probably just as well. "And the sticker's torn."

"You could see that while the bike was going at high speed?"

"Are you kidding me? I'll be seeing it for weeks in my nightmares. I had a clear view of the sticker when the bike turned to have another go at me."

After I'd signed my printed statement and the recorder was turned off, he said, "We got preliminaries back on the body found in Martin Hodgins's home."

I dreaded what was coming next, even though I had to hear it. Poor Gemma. "And?"

He shook his head. "The remains are not those of Martin Hodgins."

Finally, some good news. I smiled at him. "Really? That's fantastic. Gemma's dad isn't dead."

Ian didn't look as thrilled as I was. "Lucy, Martin Hodgins is nowhere to be found. He's a person of interest in our inquiries."

"What?" My euphoria was immediately doused. I was pretty sure that 'person of interest' was Brit cop speak for 'the guy we think did the deed.' I almost thought it would be easier for Gemma if her father had been murdered than if he turned out to have caused a death. "So, you're saying the man didn't die of natural causes?"

"That depends on what you consider natural causes. He died of smoke inhalation and then his body burned in the fire. But that fire wasn't accidental."

My head was spinning. Both my pet theories, one, that Darren had killed Gemma's dad, and two, that Sanderson had killed Gemma's dad, were wrong. Not only was Gemma's dad not dead, but the police didn't know who was.

CHAPTER 17

"Oh, no. Poor Gemma." I sat, slumped in my chair, feeling like a gray fog was pulling at me.

"Darren was on his way to see Martin Hodgins. I'm convinced of it. He said he was going there when he left Oxford. I'm telling you, he's deranged. He nearly murdered Gemma and today he rode his motorcycle straight at me. He must have done it."

Ian sat back. He was looking at me as though I were a fellow detective and we were colleagues discussing a case. It was so cool. "I'm listening. Why would Gemma's ex-boyfriend try and kill someone at his ex-girlfriend's father's home?"

Okay, so this chummy detective thing wasn't as easy as it looked on TV. I tried to form some kind of theory that made sense. "He'd never seen her father, so when he saw a man at the house, he assumed it was Martin Hodgins and killed him."

"Why?"

"I don't know. Why would he try and kill his ex-girlfriend?"

Ian looked at me like I was being dull witted. "Because he was jealous and angry and rejected. But to kill her father, who's all but estranged from his daughter, doesn't fit any profile I've ever heard of."

He had a point. But, since Darren had driven his motorcycle at me like a killing machine, I was quite happy to add every crime imaginable to his rap sheet.

"They hadn't been going out very long. Maybe he didn't know she and her dad were estranged." I shrugged. I was reaching, but if I could talk through my fuzzy theory maybe it would sharpen into focus. "They shared a surname. How hard could it be to track the man down?"

He didn't look as though he completely believed me, but Ian wasn't interrupting either. He was listening.

I got up. It helped me to pace, even though there wasn't much space in the small room. "He planned to talk to Martin Hodgins. Tell him why he and Gemma were meant to be together." I snapped my fingers and it sounded like a pebble hitting glass. "Gemma told me he'd already planned when they'd get married and have their first kid. I bet he went to her father to ask for her hand in marriage."

Ian looked like a wasp had stung him. "Do people still do that?"

Since my father had never been troubled by offers for my hand, I really couldn't say. "I have no idea, but Darren was not like most men. He was obsessed with Gemma. He seriously had their whole future mapped out. When she broke up with him he threatened to kill himself. I'm telling you, this guy is not playing with a full deck."

"All right. Let's assume you're correct and Darren went to

Martin Hodgins's home to ask for her hand. Then, what happened?"

My theory was seriously vague at this point. I gnawed my thumbnail. I stared at the floor, noting a black scuff mark that made me wonder if there'd been a violent tussle in this room at some point. I pictured a perp, or maybe cop, pushed up against the wall.

I turned. "You're absolutely certain the dead body's not Martin Hodgins?"

He looked much less serious when he was trying not to smirk. "The labs don't usually make mistakes like that. It's not Hodgins. Though, as yet, we don't know who it is. No hits yet from crime databases."

Chewing my thumbnail wasn't helping, and it was ruining my manicure, so I stopped. "Maybe Darren banged on the door and whoever was in the house said he wasn't Martin Hodgins, but Darren didn't believe them. He thought it was Gemma's father and he was lying. He was so enraged he killed the guy. Then staged a fire to cover the evidence."

"Ah, yes, and speaking of evidence..."

I blew out a breath. "There isn't any. I know. But it's possible, right?"

"Many things are possible, Lucy. But we can't make arrests based on 'possible.'" Before the words piling up in my throat could burst out, he put up a hand. "But, we certainly have sufficient reason to pick him up in connection with the attack on you."

"Then you lean on him. Tell him you know he killed Gemma's father." I thought of that high-strung, intense guy who'd obviously lost the plot and badly. "I bet he'll crumble and confess."

"We can always hope."

Then Ian stood as well, indicating that we were done. He held the door for me and as I walked out, he said, "In the meantime, I don't want you going out alone. And make sure you always have an assistant in the shop with you."

"You think I'm in danger?" It was a stupid question, obviously, as I knew the second I said the words out loud. *Yeah, Lucy, guys running motorcycles at you generally aren't asking for a date.* I shook my head. "Never mind."

He stopped me with a hand on my arm. "We'll find him. But, until we do, stay vigilant. Promise me?"

It was one of those moments fraught with too many things unsaid. I nodded.

For now, it was enough.

Violet dropped me off at home and offered to come in with me. I could tell she was worried, but I reminded her that Meri was there. I'd be fine.

When I got up to the flat, I saw that Rafe was also there, looking furious and pacing up and down. Nyx was in his arms, and I got the feeling that Nyx would've done her own pacing if she didn't have Rafe to do it for her.

The minute I was inside, he put down the cat and stalked forward, grabbed my shoulders. "I just heard. Are you all right?"

I'd heard that line quite a few times in the last couple of hours. "Yes. I'm fine. It was terrifying in the moment, but I stopped him." I could let Violet think I'd managed the protection spell on my own, but I wouldn't lie to Rafe. "Actually, Nyx sent me a spell and it worked. Luckily."

He shook his head, looking fond and frustrated as he

often did when he looked at me. "I cannot let you out of my sight."

"I did find out one interesting thing."

"That Darren is back? There are more subtle ways to gather information, Lucy."

I shook my head at him, impatient. "Something else. The man who died in that fire wasn't Martin Hodgins."

He looked at me, an arrested expression on his face. "Really? Do they know who the dead person was?"

"No. Not yet."

He'd been around a lot longer than I had and, I suspected, was much smarter. He didn't get all excited about the news that Martin Hodgins was still alive. He'd done the mental route finding and got to the part where Gemma's dad was the likely suspect in the death of whoever the charred corpse was in his house. "Have they found Martin Hodgins yet?"

"I don't think so." I picked up Nyx since she was circling around my ankles so tightly she was a tripping hazard. She settled against me, purring. "If we hadn't just seen Dominic Sanderson in the flesh last night, I'd been tempted to think it was him in that fire. It would be a nice twist on the Shakespearean tragedy where the old friend goes to visit the man he's betrayed intending to murder him. But, instead of the man whose life's work he stole, dying, he's the one who ends up dead."

"That would be very satisfying on stage. Sadly, as you say, we know the dead man wasn't Dominic Sanderson."

"Could it have been an emissary? Or, I don't know, a hitman?"

"It could be any number of people. There's not much

point in speculating. We'll know the identity of the victim soon enough."

And, knowing Rafe, he'd know before Ian did.

CHAPTER 18

I went to see Gemma the following day. Her condition was stable, and the doctors had eased up on her visiting restrictions. When I went in, both Clara and Mabel were sitting by her bedside. Clara was holding Gemma's hand and speaking to her softly, while Mabel sat in the corner knitting. I was pleased to see that Mabel was holding her knitting speed down to that of an extremely proficient mortal. I thought, if she knitted at her usual speed and anyone saw her, they'd either run for their lives or admit her into the hospital for testing. Neither outcome would be very good.

Both the vampires looked delighted to see me. Clara got up and insisted that I take her seat beside the bed. She whispered, "I'm certain that her hand felt warmer today than it did yesterday."

I had no idea if that was good, but I hoped so. Unless she was running a fever or something but then presumably the machines would've caught that. I looked at Gemma's peaceful face and said, "Gemma, I wish you would wake up. I have so much I want to say to you. The holiday market's not the same without you."

Her hand did seem warm and after I'd babbled on for a couple more minutes, I felt her fingers stir within mine. I gasped and turned to look at the two vampires. Clara had also pulled out her knitting, now, and neither of them were watching me. I lowered my voice and said, urgently, "She moved her fingers."

They both put down their knitting and rose out of their seats and drew closer. "Are you sure?" Clara whispered.

Now I wasn't so sure. "I think so."

I felt it again, not strong but definitely. "She did it again. She's gripping my fingers."

"That's excellent," Mabel said. "Keep talking to her."

Now, of course, my mind went blank. I couldn't think of a thing to say to the poor woman. I couldn't tell her that her father's house had burned down, and someone inside was dead, not her father, though that probably made him the chief suspect. No one waking from a coma wanted to hear that.

I could also tell her that her ex-boyfriend, the creepy stalker, had tried to run me down on the street. No one wanted to wake up out of a coma and hear that, either.

I said, "I've been thinking, Gemma, when you wake up, you should learn how to knit. It's very soothing." I have no idea why I said that. Knitting was never soothing to me, but I thought, maybe, to Gemma it might be. She was clearly a crafty person since she could make soap, scented bath salts, and creams and things.

"Don't like knitting."

Three of us in the room gasped and looked at each other,

wondering who had said it. Clara and Mabel both loved knitting and were happily engaged in it at the moment. I was the one who didn't like knitting and I hadn't said the words. That only left one other possibility. We all stared at Gemma. Her eyes were still closed, and her voice had been weak, but unless we were all three sharing an auditory hallucination, Gemma had spoken.

Mabel said, "Should we get a doctor?"

I shook my head. "Not yet. Give her a minute before the white coats start crowding in on her."

They nodded and we all perched on the edge of our chairs staring at Gemma.

Nothing happened. I said, "You've had a good, long, sleep. Gemma, it's time to wake up. There's so much I have to tell you. Besides, we just started getting to know each other and becoming friends. I don't have very many friends in Oxford. Or in England. Or anywhere come to that. Please open your eyes."

I was convinced her eyelashes fluttered and then she said, "They feel heavy."

I looked at the other two. "Oh, that time she definitely spoke to me. And she clearly understands what I'm saying to her."

"Who are you talking to?" Gemma asked in a somewhat querulous tone.

I thought I might start crying. I definitely felt tears pricking my lashes. "These two ladies are strangers to you, but they've been sitting with you every day, so you'd never feel lonely."

Gemma made a noise and muttered a few words. I thought she was falling back into a deep sleep but then, suddenly, her eyes opened. She looked around, somewhat confused, and then her gaze settled on my face. "Lucy. I thought I heard your voice. What are you doing here?" Her voice was a little croaky, but her words were completely lucid.

She looked around again. "What is this place? Am I in the hospital?"

The tears were running freely down my face. "You are. You're in the hospital. You had an accident, but I think you're going to be fine." I wiped my wet cheeks with the back of my free hand.

"My throat's dry. Can I have some water?"

"Of course." I couldn't bear to let go of her hand. "Clara, perhaps you could get Gemma some water and tell the doctor the good news."

But some mysterious machine must've already sent out an alert, for a nurse came bustling in. "Oh, bless her, she's awake."

She said it in a hearty tone that made Gemma wince. She checked the machines and then said, "I'm fetching the doctor now, my love. But I'm afraid your visitors will have to leave."

She made shooing motions to us. I was about to let go of Gemma's hand, but Gemma gripped it. "I want Lucy to stay," she said.

Nurse looked as though she was going to argue, but, at that moment Dr. Patek came in. He must've overheard Gemma's words for he said, "Of course, Lucy can stay. We're very glad to see you awake. How are you feeling?"

Gemma looked from me to him and said, "I don't remember what happened. Did someone hit me?"

I looked at the doctor. Let him handle this one. He said,

"Let's start with how you're feeling. Do you have pain anywhere?"

She seemed to think about it. "I'm thirsty. I want some water."

Dr. Patek chuckled. "That's easy to remedy. Nurse? Our patient would like some water."

"Of course, Dr. Patek," she said and bustled back out again.

Clara and Mabel had left, so it was only the three of us in the room. Dr. Patek picked up her chart and then he took out a ballpoint pen. "Can you tell me your name?"

"Gemma Andrea Hodgins."

"Excellent. What's your date of birth, Gemma?"

"June 13, 1988." He noted something. "Do you know what the season is?"

"Unless I've been hibernating, it's still winter." She looked at me, suddenly uncertain, "Isn't it?"

I nodded. She was doing so well. A complete recovery was almost more than I'd dared to hope. He asked her some more questions and made her follow his finger with her eyes. "Excellent," he said, looking pleased. "Excellent."

The water arrived in a plastic lidded cup with a straw, and the nurse helped Gemma sit up. There was an IV drip in her arm, that she glanced at with suspicion. She drank a few sips of water and then put a hand to her bruised throat. I could almost feel her memories coming back. She began to tremble. "I remember now. I was at the holiday market. Somebody attacked me. They tried to strangle me." She looked at me. "Didn't they?"

I didn't glance at the doctor because I didn't want to see if he shook his head. I was not going to lie to Gemma. If I was in her position, I'd want to know the truth. "Yes. Someone did attack you. Did you see who it was?"

She closed her eyes and I almost begged her not to. I was frightened she'd slip back into unconsciousness. But, after a few seconds, she opened them, slowly, then shook her head. "I couldn't see anything." She put a hand to her throat. "I thought I was going to die!"

I held onto her hand. "It's okay. You're safe."

She looked at me, her eyes wide and frightened in her pale face. The bruises on her neck were vivid blues, yellows, and purples. "Am I?"

Between the police and the vampires she was as safe as we could make her. I nodded.

She looked around the room and out of the open door into the corridor where an orderly was pushing a patient past in a wheelchair. It was an old man with wisps of white on his head, like scattered cloud. He was bent over in his blue hospital gown so his back barely touched the chair. Her eyes swept to the window, looking out on gray clouds. "I don't feel safe. Where's my dad? Is he here?"

I had no idea what to say. I went with, "I'm not sure if he's been informed."

She seemed to be thinking. "Perhaps it's for the best."

A strange looking older guy wandered past the open door. He had straggly gray-brown curls brushing the collar of an old woolen jacket, an ancient pair of jeans that were too big and a woolen cap on his head. He glanced up and down the halls as though frightened of being discovered. He held a duffel bag against his chest as though it contained all his worldly possessions. My first thought was that a homeless man had somehow wandered in. Then, Gemma followed my gaze. "Dad?" She blinked a few times as though she didn't trust her senses.

The man turned and came in. His blue eyes filled with tears as he came toward the bed, with eyes for no one but Gemma. "My baby," he said. "What have they done to you?"

"Daddy!" she squeaked and held out her arms, wincing when she pulled on the IV.

He came forward and hugged her awkwardly, the tears running down his face now. So this was Martin Hodgins.

I let go of Gemma's hand and prepared to leave father and daughter to their reunion, but Gemma stopped me. "Lucy, don't go. I want you to meet my dad. Martin Hodgins, this is Lucy Swift. She's been a good friend to me."

He patted me around the duffel bag. "Thank you."

Dr. Patek said he'd come back later and I said I would, too, but Gemma insisted I stay. "I need to tell you something," she said. "I think I know who attacked me."

CHAPTER 19

"What?" I cried.

"Of course you do," her father agreed, making me stare at him. "Same evil viper who tried to kill me."

"What?" I repeated. My voice grew more shrill with each outburst.

Gemma leaned back onto her pillows. She sipped more water.

"I put you in danger," Martin Hodgins said. "I'll never forgive myself. You're all I have left, all I care about. What's a book compared to you?"

She shook her head and I noticed her eyes were swimming now. "I put myself in danger. I didn't think it through properly. I thought I could make him do the right thing. I told him I had proof."

"Who?" I asked, though I suspected I knew.

"Sanderson, of course," Martin answered.

Gemma nodded. "I phoned him, you see. I called Professor Sanderson and told him I had proof that Dad was the real author of the Chronicles of Pangnirtung." She sighed and looked at me. "Lucy won't understand what we're talking about, but my father wrote the Chronicles. He and Sanderson were at school together, and—"

I was worried she was tiring herself out, so I interrupted. "I do know. You hinted at the story when we had dinner in the pub and, while you've been in hospital, I've been doing some research."

Father and daughter both stared at me. "You have?" she asked.

"Why would you do that?" he wanted to know. He pulled the duffel bag closer to his chest. Poor man, after all these years I could see that his experience of being betrayed had led to near paranoia.

"Because Gemma and I are friends." I paused. Why had I launched myself, yet again, into other people's business? It was becoming a bad habit. "Because I can't stand seeing injustice."

He looked from me to Gemma. "You trust her? She could be—"

"I trust her, Dad. It wasn't Lucy who attacked me. It was Sanderson."

That dry, dusty professor didn't look like a murderer, but I supposed when driven to desperation, he'd done what he believed he had to in order to keep his secrets safe.

However, I'd recently been grilled by Ian and I knew how important it was for the police to get accurate evidence. "Did you see Sanderson attack you?" I asked.

The both stared at me again. Then Gemma shook her head. "No. I didn't. I was in the chalet, closing up. I heard something move behind me and when I tried to turn he grabbed me around the throat. I never saw him. But it was the same day I'd phoned Sanderson. Who else could it have been?"

"What about Darren? He kept hanging around, bothering you." I had to remind her.

"Darren? You think he could have done this?" She touched her throat.

"I don't know, but maybe we shouldn't jump to conclusions. Sanderson stole your father's manuscript, but it happened forty years ago. Why would he suddenly turn murderous now?"

"Because I found the damned manuscript," Martin Hodgins said.

For the third time, I said, "What?"

He looked sheepish. "I have to take you back to my days at college. I'd finished the trilogy. No one knew anything about it but Sanders. He'd read early drafts, encouraged me. He'd argue with me about key points and we'd drink and talk late into the night. Then, toward the end of that year, he began to act peculiar. He started calling it 'our' book. He'd certainly read parts of it and talked through some of the plot points, but it was always my series. I tinkered with it constantly. I even kept the pages in a cardboard box beside my bed."

"You kept the only copy of the Chronicles of Pangnirtung in a box beside your bed?" I asked in a faint voice. I thought of all the things that could have happened to it. Fire, theft, water damage, a drunk undergrad could have thrown up on those precious pages.

He made a sound like a snort. "Didn't know its value, then, did I?"

He glanced at the door as though expecting trouble. But

there was no one there. "One day it went missing. Sanders said he'd borrowed it, wanted to give the whole series a read. He knew I was getting ready to send it to a publisher."

"He stole it from under your nose?"

"Pretty much. Said he was giving it a final read and he'd give it back to me the following week. Don't know why I didn't believe him. But, I thought he was up to something. But, I'd been burning the candle at both ends, writing my final essay for our Old English class and working on the book. Hadn't had enough sleep. Thought I was being paranoid."

"Did Sanderson offer to hand in your paper for you?" I asked.

He goggled at me. "How in blazes could you know that?"

"Because he obviously tampered with it, that's why you were accused of plagiarism."

He nodded. "You're right, of course. The viper. I was so stunned about the charges, and here was he, pretending to be my friend, feeding me beer, telling me it would all be all right. I asked for the manuscript and he claimed he'd taken it to his parents' home for the final read and left it there." He shook his head. "I didn't believe him, but my first priority was to fight the plagiarism charges. I know it's hard to believe, looking back, but I cared more about my degree than the pile of manuscript pages. When I lost the appeal and got sent down, I didn't handle it well. Started drinking."

"So, once he'd discredited you, he felt safe in presenting the manuscript as his own."

"He was devious. Clever. When I went to pick up my belongings from my lodgings, he'd gone through the place. I could tell. Every bit of scrap paper was missing. He'd emptied waste paper baskets, picked through my belongings. To the casual observer, the place looked exactly as I'd left it, but I knew he'd cleared out every hint of that manuscript." His voice was bitter and low. I felt he was reliving the fierce burn of betrayal all over again.

But I'd seen manuscript pages in Gemma's hotel room. And the way he was clutching that duffel bag I didn't think it contained his washing. "But you had a copy, didn't you?"

His eyes narrowed, briefly, on my face. Then he chuckled. "I'd made a copy for my dad to read. Never bothered to tell Sanders. Why would I?"

"So, there was a complete copy of the manuscript at your parents' home?"

He closed his eyes as though he'd experienced a sharp pain. "Dad wasn't a tidy man, you have to understand, but Mum was always tidying. She did a clean up of all his rubbish, as she called it and said she'd boxed everything up and put it in the attic. I couldn't find the box. Wasn't until they died that I found the manuscript in a box labeled Insurance." He chuckled. "Apt in a way."

"You mean that when you challenged Sanderson and said you'd written the books, you didn't actually have the copy."

"No." He looked uncomfortable. "I thought I could shame him into admitting the truth, but the man's shameless. If anyone had investigated properly, I could have shown my research, explained where I'd come up with the characters and the world. Sanderson couldn't explain anything, because he hadn't created it. But they treated me like a joke." I could feel his hurt and had to remember that he'd been younger than I was when all this had happened. He'd believed justice would prevail.

Gemma didn't know about the fire, or the body found in his house, so I didn't know how to bring it up. Was it possible that Martin Hodgins had finally taken the law into his own hands and, knowing his daughter had been attacked, and got justice on his own terms?

He continued with his story. "My wife always said she believed me, but I couldn't let it rest. The betrayal was like a canker sore in my heart, always spilling poison into every aspect of my life. I tried to move on. I worked as a teacher, that's how we met. But I drank too much, and after a time, she couldn't take it anymore. I understood, of course, but once I lost my family, I lost all hope."

"Oh, Dad."

"It wasn't your mother's fault. I know it was partly my own, but of course, the real villain was Sanderson. I'd go along and be all right, and then there'd be another movie of *my story* come out. Sanders would be on the telly talking about *his* books and I'd feel such a helpless rage that I'd bury myself in a bottle."

He shook his head. "Not much of a role model, was I?"

"You did your best, Dad."

"When my mum died and I went through all the papers, I found the box with my manuscript in it. I didn't know what to do with it. Gemma's mum was sick by that time, so I put it in a storage lock-up with some old furniture of my Mum and Dad's."

"What a good thing you did," I said, thinking of his house fire.

He nodded. "After her mum died, Gemma and I spent more time together." He looked at his daughter. "I didn't want you to think your old dad was nothing but a worthless drunk."

"I'd never think that."

"I wanted you to know what I'd been capable of. Once." He patted the duffel. "So, I took the first couple of chapters over and gave them to her."

Gemma took up the story now. "When I realized that Dad had actual proof he was the author of the Chronicles, I was determined to get him the recognition he deserved." She looked at me. "He's got everything. The old books he used for his research, lists of Inuit words he drew from in naming his people and creatures. Old maps and diaries of fur traders in the north of Canada, in what's now called Nunavut."

She looked at her father. "When all you had was those books and source materials, it wasn't enough, but with your manuscript, I was positive we could get someone to listen to us. I even talked to a journalist friend. But, since Dad had already been in the news and not been taken seriously, he didn't think there was much he could do. I was so angry, I decided to go to Oxford myself. The craft market gave me a good excuse. Besides, I did need the money. But I chose Oxford so I could confront Sanderson with the proof of what he'd done. I wanted to force him to do the right thing." She touched her throat. "Not a smart decision."

"You spoke to him?"

"Yes. I phoned him. I told him I had the manuscript. He asked me to give him a couple of days." She shut her eyes. "He sounded so harmless on the phone. He asked when and where we could meet and I told him I was working at the holiday market so it would have to be once the market was over." She opened her eyes again but she glared up at the ceiling. "I was so stupid. All he had to do was kill me and take the manuscript."

Her father reached for her hand. "He tried to kill me, too."

"Oh, Dad, no. Whatever have I done? I was only trying to help you."

Before they both wallowed in more self blame, I said, "How did Sanderson try to kill you, Mr. Hodgins?"

"The police had come to the door that morning to tell me Gemma was in the hospital." He swallowed. "They told me she'd been attacked and I knew who'd done it." His teeth snapped together. "I don't care what happens to me. I'm old and broken down, but he was going to pay for what he'd done to my daughter."

Oh, dear. I wasn't sure I wanted to hear this part. Or that I wanted Gemma to, but I was powerless to stop him now he'd begun his tale. "I put all my source materials in the storage locker. I made another copy of the manuscript and stored that away safely, too." He patted the duffel bag. "This is the original in here. All but the chapters Gemma has." I didn't correct him. There'd be time to explain later that Rafe actually had them safe.

"I've decided. I'm going to go public again with my claims. I'm older now, I don't drink anymore, and I've got the manuscript. This time, they'll listen to me. Nobody hurts my baby girl and gets away with it. I'll take Sanderson down, if it's the last thing I do. Why, losing his reputation, his job, all his money, and being exposed as the lying fraud he is? That will be a fate worse than death for my old friend Sanders. He'll end up in jail. More of a broken man than I ever was."

This was great, but I wanted to go back to the part where he thought Sanderson had tried to kill him. "How did the professor try to kill you?" There were no strangulation marks on his throat and he seemed to be uninjured.

"I was coming back to my place to pack a few clothes and head down here to the hospital. I was walking down the road and I heard some kind of explosion. Then I saw the flames. In my own house. I started forward and then saw him come running out. He'd set the fire. Tried to kill me. He got on his motorbike and rode away."

Gemma put her hand in her father's and they clutched each other, obviously both thinking of their lucky escapes.

"This man who got on the motorcycle, did you see his face?"

"No. He had a helmet on. But who but Sanderson would want me dead? And a fire would destroy any books or papers, wouldn't it?"

"Was the motorcycle black?"

"Yes."

I shook my head. "I don't think that was Sanderson. I think the man you saw running away from the burning building was Gemma's ex."

They both stared at me. Gemma said, "Darren?"

"Yes. Darren told me he was going to see your father. He was very angry. And he rides a black motorbike."

"But, but that's impossible," Gemma said.

A new voice spoke up from the doorway. "I'm happy to see that you're awake, Gemma."

It was Ian. They must have called to let him know Gemma was awake and talking. She looked at him, puzzled. "You're a friend of Lucy's, aren't you?"

She'd only met him the once and had been rude about his purchase of the fortieth edition of the Chronicles. I hadn't bothered to tell her he was a police officer. Now, I did. "Gemma, this is Detective Inspector Ian Chisholm."

He walked into the room. He looked very official in a jacket and tie though, as usual, his wavy hair was unruly. It looked as though some woman had just run her hands through it. He said, "Gemma's right. It is impossible that it was Darren you saw leaving your property, Mr. Hodgins. Darren's charred body was found in the house."

CHAPTER 20

"*D*arren's dead?" Gemma asked in a whisper.

"I'm afraid so."

It was my turn to say, "But that's impossible." I stared at Ian. "Have you forgotten that Darren tried to run me over?"

"From what I overheard, neither Mr. Hodgins, or you, saw the face of this motorcycle rider."

I felt as though I'd just worked for days on one of those jigsaw puzzles with five gazillion little pieces, and the last few wouldn't fit. "But, it was Darren's bike. I told you, I recognized that decal."

Gemma made a funny sound. "Babe Magnet?"

I nodded. "See?"

"I'm not saying it wasn't Darren's bike that tried to run you down, what I'm saying is that Darren wasn't driving it."

"Then who was?"

"Sanderson," Martin Hodgins said. "Must have been."

Ian looked at me with raised eyebrows. I knew he trusted me to tell him the truth as I knew it. I looked at Gemma. "Is it okay if

I fill Ian in on what you were telling me?" I didn't want her to tire herself out unnecessarily. She nodded, looking weary. Quickly, I related the story she'd told me. I explained about the manuscript, that she'd spoken to Sanderson and told him she had the manuscript and could prove her father's authorship."

I could see that Ian was almost more interested in this than in his murder investigation. He put up a hand. "Wait." He looked at Martin Hodgins. "Can you really prove that you wrote the Chronicles?"

"I can." He unzipped the duffel bag and pulled out a few pages. "You can see my scribbled notes in the margins. I've got all my source materials." While Ian looked at the papers with a slightly stunned expression, Martin Hodgins dug to the bottom of the bag. "Wait, this is the best of all. I'd actually forgotten all about it."

He rummaged and it sounded like he was scratching through fallen leaves. Then he said, "Here it is," and pulled out a large envelope. He pulled out the contents, cleared his throat and read, "Dear Mr. Hodgins. Thank you for submitting your trilogy of fantasy novels, The Chronicles of Pangnirtung to our publisher for consideration. Unfortunately, while we enjoyed aspects of the novels, we do not feel we can accept your novels for publication. We wish you success in your literary endeavors." He waved the pages about. "It is dated six months before Sanderson presented the novels as his own. And, since I'd sent a self-addressed stamped envelope, the publisher kindly returned my pages, with notations."

Ian handed back the pages he'd been looking at. "Sir, if your claims are true, and I'm beginning to believe they are, then may I be the first of your fans to apologize for what's been done to you?"

"You can," said Martin Hodgins. "And when I get them published under my own name, I'll sign a set for you."

"We've gone off topic," I reminded Ian. "The point is, that Gemma spoke to Dominic Sanderson and told him she had her father's manuscript. He told her he was willing to meet. She informed him she had a stall at the holiday market. She was strangled later that day at the holiday market."

He had his cop face on, now. When I'd finished speaking, he said to Gemma, "Did you see him?"

She shook her head.

"All right. You rest up. I'm very glad you're all right." He walked out into the corridor and I followed him.

"Ian. Aren't you going to arrest Sanderson? What more does he have to do? Walk around with a sign saying, "I did it?"

"You should do us both a favor and apply to join the force. Oh, wait, you can't. You're American. What a shame." He turned and took a step toward the exit.

"Ian!"

He turned back. "I'm going to bring him in for questioning, all right?"

I knew he had to follow proper police procedure, but at least he was getting that man off the streets before he could attempt to harm Gemma or her father again. "I'm worried about my friend, that's all."

He relented and came toward me. "I know you are. And when this is all over—"

His phone chimed and he pulled it out of his pocket. He frowned and picked up. "DI Chisholm."

He listened. "Right." Then his eyes widened and for some reason he looked up at me. "I'll be right there."

"What?" I asked when he rang off.

He said, slowly, "Dominic Sanderson was found dead in his home. He hanged himself." We were both silent and then he shook his head. "He wrote the final chapter of his life his own way."

And then he turned and walked away.

CHAPTER 21

To my complete surprise, Gemma reopened Bubbles. She'd been released from hospital and her father had picked her up in a limousine and taken her, not back to her rented room in Botley, but to a suite in the Randolph, one of the best hotels in Oxford.

I walked down to the market with yet another set of stockings for Timeless Treasures and saw that Bubbles was open and busy. Gemma wore a green turtle neck sweater to hide the fading bruises, but otherwise she looked as though she'd never been hurt. Mabel had knitted it for her specially. Since they'd spent so much time looking after her she'd decreed they were her honorary aunties. Even though Dr. Patek had given her a clean bill of health, I was still surprised to see her working so soon. Even more shocking, she had a helper.

Martin Hodgins was busy making change and wrapping soaps. He looked like a different, younger version of himself. His hair was freshly cut, he wore a brand new cream woolen shirt that I suspected Gemma had picked out, a tweed jacket, and jeans that actually fit. He was never going to be the life and soul of the party, but he seemed like a kind and gentle introvert rather than a bitter, broken one.

I walked over and gave her a hug. "Gemma, I can't believe you're back."

She stepped out of the booth and we walked a few steps away where we could talk without being overheard. She gave me a wry smile. "I had to do it, Lucy. I had to come and finish what I started. Sanderson ruined enough of our lives, I wasn't going to let his attack stop me from completing my time at the market. Besides, I was getting bored sitting around in that fancy hotel. How many spa treatments and fancy meals can one woman have?"

I sighed, imagining. "I'd like to take that challenge and find out."

She laughed. "It's been amazing. Everything is changing for us. Sanderson's agent, Charles Beach, came down from London when he heard what had happened. He and Dad had a long talk. He gave Dad a hefty advance on future earnings. Enough for us to stay in the Randolph. He's going to represent Dad."

My eyebrows shot up. "Your dad didn't want his own agent?"

She glanced at her father, who seemed to be coping fine, and said, "At first, he did, but Charles convinced him he was the best person for the job. He knows the books better than anyone and he's already proven he can sell them. Plus, the best part is, that because he's representing Dad, that's all the proof of authorship anyone needs. It helps us avoid lengthy legal battles that Dad's just not up for. Chaz is working up new contracts so my dad and the publishers make the money and not the lawyers."

That sounded like something call-me-Chaz would say. "I'm so glad it's worked out so well for everyone."

"I think Dad would have liked his day in court. He feels a bit cheated, in a way, that Sanderson took the easy way out."

There was a kind of irony in Dominic Sanderson's end. He'd tried to strangle Gemma to death and ended up strangling himself. I didn't say that, though, it seemed a bit macabre.

She laughed. "I feel like we got a Christmas miracle."

"I'm so glad. You deserve it. You both do."

"I'd better get back, but Dad and I want you to come for dinner tonight at the hotel. You've done so much for us. And the food's amazing."

"I'd love to."

It was almost impossible to believe that everything had worked out so well. I was wearing a beautiful red sweater that Clara had knit. It was the one she'd been working on while she'd sat by Gemma's bed all those hours. It kept me warm and, since the sun was out and I was in no hurry to head back to Cardinal Woolsey's, I thought I'd do some Christmas shopping.

I couldn't resist buying a box of chocolates for Ian. They were meant for children, I imagined, but they were decorated with British police bobby hats. As I turned away, I bumped into Ian himself. "Hello," I said in surprise.

"Lucy." Ian looked pleased to see me. "I was coming to the knitting stall to find you."

I started to form a question and then stopped myself.

He shook his head at me. "What is it? If you've got questions, I'll try and answer them."

"It's just that I still can't figure out how Darren ended up dead?"

He pulled me aside so we were out of the crowd. "Darren did go to Martin Hodgins' house. It seems he told several people he was going there, not only you. He seems to have believed her father could influence Gemma and get her to go out with him again. This is just a theory, mind you, but we believe he surprised Sanderson in the act of setting fire to Martin Hodgins' home. No doubt Sanderson had hidden his car somewhere nearby and when Darren kept banging on the door and making a fuss, shouting, "Hodgins, I know you're in there," which several neighbors confirm he did, Sanderson let him in and pretended to be Hodgins. He bashed him over the head with the brick he'd used to break in, and then set fire to the place."

I hadn't liked Darren, but that was a horrible end for anyone. "And then Sanderson stole his helmet and motorbike to get away. So it looked like Darren arrived and left."

"Exactly."

"He really was a cold-blooded killer. Darren hadn't done anything to him."

"Except show up at a most inopportune moment."

"So it was Sanderson who tried to run me down."

"We believe so."

"But why kill me? I hadn't done anything."

"I've been wondering that myself. I suspect that your interview with Professor Naylor got back to him."

I shot a glance at him under my lashes. "You know about that?"

He nodded. I knew he wanted to scold me but it seemed he couldn't be bothered to waste his breath. "Professor Naylor was very forthcoming. I interviewed him as part of a routine inquiry into Sanderson's suicide. He mentioned a graduate student from the USA had interviewed him and been particularly interested in the old scandal. Naturally, he'd told Sanderson."

"How do you know it was me? There must be loads of grad students who come over from the States."

"Lucy, you used your real name."

"Oh." I thought about it. "So, Sanderson tried to kill me because I was asking questions?"

"No. I think he was after the manuscript."

My eyes widened. "My carry bag. I dropped it when I fell."

"You told me it had the packing slips in it. Since Sanderson hadn't found the manuscript when he searched Gemma's room, and he knew you were asking questions, he probably put two and two together. He saw you walking along with a bag of papers and decided to grab them. Remember, by that point, he was a very desperate man."

"I almost feel sorry for him. Almost."

"You should feel sorry for yourself."

I gulped. "Why?"

He opened his mouth, then looked at me and sighed. "In the seasonal spirit of good will, I'm going to refrain from asking how you knew Gemma had that manuscript, and what you've done with it."

I thought that was an excellent decision on his part. "Good. Because I just bought you a Christmas present."

His eyes twinkled when he looked at me. "Did you? You'd better give it to me now, then."

"Why? Christmas is days away."

"Because I'm going to Scotland for the holidays, leaving this afternoon. My sister had a baby and wants me to go." He shrugged and looked a little uncomfortable. He wasn't big on sharing personal stuff.

"All right." I gave him the box of chocolates and when he saw the little decorated hats he chuckled. Then opened the box and offered me one. We both took a sweet and bit into it. Oh, they were good. He looked at me, with laughter in his eyes and said, "Come here, I've got something for you, too."

He took my arm and pulled me behind a chalet selling wreaths and artificial trees and ornaments. It was relatively quiet and I looked up at him, expecting him to give me a silly gift. Instead, he pointed above my head. "Mistletoe," he said.

I looked up. "That's not mistletoe. That's plastic ivy," I protested, but my heart started to pound.

"My mistake," he said, and leaning forward, kissed me. He tasted like chocolate and promise. I pulled back, startled and blushing. He was smiling down at me. "Merry Christmas, Lucy."

"M-merry Christmas."

He said, "I want to see Gemma and her father before I catch my train, but I'll call you when I get back."

"Yes," I said, my lips still tingling. "Fine."

He walked back into the crowd and I took a moment to feel silly and girlish and pleased with myself. I couldn't wait for tonight. I was going to have to get Gemma alone and deconstruct this whole kissing thing and try to work out what it meant. Joke kiss? Christmas kiss? I want to marry you and have eleven children kiss? I was so bad at this. And, then there was the tiny problem of me having a hidden life. Ian already thought I was trouble, and he didn't know I was a witch.

I made my way back to Timeless Treasures.

Ian was chatting to Gemma and her father. I saw him shake the older man's hand. Then, Gemma went on serving customers and her dad came around from behind the chalet and stood to the side, chatting to Ian. To my surprise, Charles Beach walked out of the crowd and toward the two men. He wore a black leather jacket and sunglasses, like this was LA. I shook my head. Still, it was great that he was making Martin Hodgins' life easier. And that was the least he could do since he'd been actively taking bread off their table for forty years.

He stood beside Ian. With their backs to me, they were about the same height and build. There were people gathered in front of Bubbles, and another crowd of young parents in front of the chalet next door selling wooden toys. The three men stood between the two chalets. I began to feel a tingling in my fingertips.

"No," I said aloud. The black jacket, his height against the chalet. I'd only seen Lucy's attacker for a few seconds in the dark, running away, but he'd looked a lot like Charles Beach.

"Lucy? You look as though you'd seen a ghost." It was Rafe, who'd appeared at my elbow. I couldn't spare him a glance. "You knew Dominic Sanderson, didn't you?"

"Not well, but nodding acquaintances. Why?"

"Was he as tall as you?"

"Yes. Thereabouts."

The man I'd seen running away that night had not been as tall as Rafe. I pushed my packages at him. "Hold these for a second, will you?"

"Lucy?"

But I was already walking toward the trio of men. Martin Hodgins saw me first and smiled broadly. "Why, Lucy. Gemma tells me you've accepted our dinner invitation."

"I'm looking forward to it." I don't know how I kept my voice so level. Ian and Charles Beach both turned as I joined the group. "Hello, Mr. Beach," I said.

His eyes shifted away. "Hello," he said, as though he didn't have a clue who I was.

"Don't you remember me?"

"I'm sorry, I don't." He patted his new client on the shoulder and said, "I'll call you Monday. We'll start setting up meetings." He turned to go.

I raised my voice. "After a man tries to run me over, I like to think he'll recognize me next time he sees me."

Ian's gaze was sharp, and Martin made a huff of surprise but Charles Beach kept on walking. He'd stiffened, so I knew he heard me.

"Mr. Beach," I all but shouted. "I saw you that night, the night you strangled Gemma. But you know that. You saw me first. And you ran. That's why you tried to kill me, to shut me up."

He turned and tried to look nonchalant, even though a lot of people at the market were staring. "I don't have time for hysterical females. I have to get back to London."

Ian glanced at me and I nodded. He stepped forward, looking as tough and cop-like as a man can who has a smear of chocolate on his lower lip. "Mr. Beach, I'll need you to come to the station and answer a few questions."

Charles Beach then did a very foolish thing. He sprinted between the chalets, trying to run away.

I'd had about enough of him. He was an evil man. A killer

who'd tried to murder my friend and helped destroy her father.

Plus, he'd called me a hysterical female, which I did not appreciate.

I didn't have Nyx feeding me the spell this time, and I didn't need her. I recited the Latin words she'd given me when I'd needed them most. I was most definitely going to fix Charles Beach's window.

Ian had taken off in hot pursuit but it wasn't long before I heard the sound I'd been waiting for. A splat, like a bug hitting a windshield on the highway. I walked between the chalets and sure enough, there was Charles Beach sprawled on the ground. Ian glanced at me as he ran by. "Did you trip him?" he asked.

"Yes."

Then, I had the pleasure of watching him arrest the man who'd caused so much trouble.

"Nicely done, Lucy," Margaret Twig said from beside me. I had no idea where she'd come from but I was gratified that she'd seen my grand performance. Lavinia was right behind her.

"Thank you."

"So, we'll be seeing you at the Winter Solstice celebration tomorrow night?"

Margaret Twig might be a much more experienced witch than I was, but I was no slouch either. I pulled myself to my full height and gave her my steeliest stare. "Only if you let me do a demonstration spell."

Lavinia looked distressed. "Oh, dear, is that a good idea?"

Margaret's thin lips curved in a smile. "I think it's a very good idea. We'll look forward to it." She nodded briskly. "Blessed be."

Rafe handed me back my packages. "How did you know it was Charles Beach?"

"I saw him standing between the chalets and my finger-tips started to tingle. And I thought, even when Gemma told me that he was going to be Martin Hodgins' agent, that it was all too neat. Everything was wrapped up like a gift ready to be put under the tree. I thought from the beginning that Dominic Sanderson wasn't a killer."

"No. He left that to his agent. They do say literary agents are sharks."

"I bet Beach killed Sanderson and it wasn't a suicide at all." I thought back, reframing what I now understood had happened. "We all kept saying how much Dominic Sanderson had to lose, but we forgot that his agent had just as much at stake." We walked together toward the Weston where the posters for the retrospective had already been removed. "Charles Beach decided to destroy Martin Hodgins' home and thereby any evidence that he'd written those books. He killed Darren simply because he was drawing attention to the house he was about to torch."

"And, then, after you'd been asking all those questions about the old scandal, he decided to kill you, as well. By that point he was in too deep to stop. When it became clear that he couldn't prevent the world from discovering that Martin Hodgins was the true author of the Chronicles, he murdered Sanderson."

"No doubt he thought the man deserved to die for misrepresenting himself to his agent."

"With his former client out of the way, he could take on

the real author and go on making money from the Chronicles."

"I feel sorry for Martin Hodgins and Gemma. They were so pleased not to have to fight to prove his authorship."

"It won't be a fight. I'll easily be able to prove the provenance of the manuscript." We sidestepped a child standing transfixed watching the lights. "I met with Martin Hodgins yesterday. He's got more than enough proof. It's just a pity it took forty years for him to get justice."

I glanced back at Gemma and her father, working happily side by side, selling soap. And I quoted Rafe's favorite author. "All's well that ends well."

Thank you for reading. I hope you enjoyed Lucy's latest adventure. Keep reading for a sneak peek of the next mystery.

A Note from Nancy

Dear Reader,

Thank you for reading the Vampire Knitting Club series. I am so grateful for all the enthusiasm this series has received. I have plenty more stories about Lucy and her undead knitters planned for the future.

I hope you'll consider leaving a review and please tell your friends who like cozy mysteries.

Review on Amazon, Goodreads or BookBub.

Your support is the wool that helps me knit up these yarns. Join my newsletter for a free prequel, *Tangles and Treasons*, the exciting tale of how the gorgeous Rafe Crosyer was turned into a vampire.

I hope to see you in my private Facebook Group. It's a lot of fun. www.facebook.com/groups/NancyWarrenKnitwits
Turn the page for a sneak peek of
Purls and Potions, Book 5 of the Vampire Knitting Club.

Until next time,
Happy Reading,

Nancy

PURLS AND POTIONS

© 2019 NANCY WARREN

Chapter 1

Frogg's Books on Harrington Street was exactly what a book-shop ought to be. The walls were lined with floor-to-ceiling bookshelves displaying novels, both popular and literary, non-fiction suitable for both Oxford students and the casual reader, and a colorful selection of children's titles. Cozy armchairs were tucked in quiet corners, inviting the customer to sit and browse.

It was across the street and up the block from Cardinal Woolsey's, the knitting and yarn shop I owned in Oxford. My cousin and part-time shop assistant Violet and I walked up with a definite purpose in mind.

We wanted to recruit Alice Robinson, the bookstore assistant, to come and teach knitting classes in my shop. I'd have taught them myself except that I was probably the worst knitter who ever owned a knitting shop. Vi could knit, but she claimed she couldn't teach.

Alice seemed like an excellent choice in a knitting

teacher. She was soft-voiced, kind and turned out beautiful work. I'd been exposed to the best, since I was so often the recipient of the gorgeous sweaters, shawls, coats and scarves knitted by my friends in the vampire knitting club that met in the back room of my shop. Still, for a living woman who hadn't had hundreds of years to perfect her craft, Alice was pretty darned good with the needles.

Also, she was nice. I'd had some shady characters end up in my shop and what I liked about Alice was that she didn't seem to be a soul-sucking demon, a murderer, or a thief. Excellent qualifications in someone working with the public.

I'd been wanting to offer knitting classes to patrons with a pulse for sometime now, but I'd wanted to find the right teacher. Since discovering that Alice had formerly taught at her last job, in a knitting shop in Somerset, I'd been keeping an eye on her. Sure, I didn't want to steal the assistant out from under the nose of Frogg's owner, Charlie Wright, but, frankly, Charlie so rarely saw what was under his nose that I doubted he'd notice if she stopped coming in.

Violet and I were doing some undercover sleuthing, feeling out whether she might be amenable to teaching classes one evening a week and on Saturday mornings. If she worked out, she'd earn some extra money and get an excellent discount on anything she purchased from Cardinal Woolsey's.

We walked into the bookstore and I took a moment to look around. I love the colorful displays of wool in Cardinal Woolseys, a patchwork of rainbow shades that make actual knitters long to buy a pattern and wool and get started. Or so they tell me. I felt the same longing when I came in here. The books all called to me, begging to be read. If I had time, I'd curl up in the empty armchair in the corner with a brand new novel and read a few pages before taking it home with me.

There were a couple of people browsing. Charlie Wright was at the counter near the back of the shop. It was the cash desk and his work area. He was seated, reading a book. I suspected he read every single volume that came through his door, sublimely unconscious of customers, noise, or boxes to be unpacked.

I knew he was thirty-four, because he'd told me when we'd chatted at the most recent meeting of our local shop owners' association. As far as I knew, he'd never been married. Like me, he lived in the flat above his shop, though I suspected his was quieter than mine, since I lived above a nest of vampires, including my grandmother, who often came to visit in the evenings.

He appeared to be a man whose friends were his books. He had thick, dark hair that flopped down on his forehead as he bent over reading. He turned a page and pushed his reading glasses up onto the bridge of his nose with his index finger.

He wore a pink shirt, though I suspected it had originally been white and got put into the wash with something red.

Alice was unpacking a box of novels onto the display table at the front of the shop. She wore her dark hair French braided and then coiled at the back, though a few wispy ringlets managed to escape and curl around her heart-shaped face. She had clear gray eyes behind large glasses, a straight nose and full lips. I'd never seen her wear cosmetics.

She hand-knitted her own cardigans and sweaters and while the work was exquisite, I always felt that she knitted the garment one size larger than necessary. All her sweaters were baggy, so she must have liked them that way. Under her sweaters she wore crisp blouses done up to the neck and longish woolen skirts with sensible low-heeled shoes. She looked like a combination between a schoolgirl and a middle-aged matron.

I guessed her to be about five years older than my own twenty-seven. Unlike the shop's owner, she'd glanced up when the bell rang announcing new customers. She put down the books she was unpacking, in a neat stack on the table, and came forward with a smile. "Lucy. Violet. How nice to see you. Are you looking for anything special or just browsing?"

She had a clear, pleasant voice and there was something comfortable about her. I knew she was the perfect choice to teach my beginner's class. I was very keen to get a good teacher as I planned to take the class myself.

"I want to talk to you," I said, "Whenever you have a minute."

She glanced around. "We're not that busy. How can I help you?"

When she looked at Charlie Wright her face grew soft with longing. No doubt she believed her feelings were known only to herself, but everyone in the neighborhood knew she was in love with Charlie. Everyone, that was, except Charlie himself.

I was extra sensitive to people's feelings, being a witch, but her yearning was so strong I could hear it, like a soulful sigh.

I explained to her that I was starting classes and I wanted her to teach them. She seemed startled by the idea and turned her gaze from Charlie to me. "Oh, I don't know. I'm very busy here."

I emphasized the hefty store discount and that we could work around Frogg's schedule.

"I don't know. I like to be available, in case Charlie needs me."

I wanted to tell her to stop being a doormat, to accept that Charlie treated her like an old and comfortable pair of slippers. But I understood a little bit about unrequited love, and so I kept my peace. "Talk it over with Charlie, and let me know," I said.

"Yes. Yes, I will. And thank you for asking me." Since we were there anyway, I decided to buy one of the novels Alice was unpacking. It looked like a very satisfying love story. Vi, meanwhile, wandered around the non-fiction shelves, emerging with a book about local herbs.

By that time, Alice was helping a grandmother choose books for her grandson's birthday. We took our purchases to the back. As I placed my book on the counter, Charlie glanced up. He blinked a few times. Charlie had gorgeous blue eyes, and a charming smile when he bothered to use it. If he'd been room décor, he'd have been shabby chic.

"Ah, Lucy, very nice to see you."

"Thank you, Charlie. Nice to see you, too."

That was the extent of our scintillating conversation. He grew more animated when he rang up Vi's purchase, telling her how much she was going to enjoy her herb book and that if she took the guide with her to the botanical gardens, she'd be able to see a number of the plants mentioned in the book. He obviously knew a lot more about local weeds and herbs than about love stories.

Alice came up, on her way to the kitchen in back. "I'll get the coffee on."

He sat back down and found his place in his book. "Lovely."

"And I made carrot cake. Your favorite."

"Yes. Excellent," he said, without looking up.

Once we were outside, Violet said, "It's an epic tragedy the way that girl pines for Charlie."

"I know. And he's so clueless. Does he even realize that she bakes him fresh cakes every day?"

"Honestly, I think you could substitute a robot with brown hair and he wouldn't notice."

"Poor Alice."

Vi stopped and put a hand on my arm. "Lucy, I've got the most marvelous idea." She sounded so enthusiastic that I grew nervous. Violet was a much more experienced witch than I and she was always pushing me to go deeper into our craft. My problem was that my magic was powerful, but not always under my control. I preferred to stick to small spells within my comfort zone.

There was a tidying up spell that I really loved.

"You remember that we talked about you working on your potions?"

Actually, she'd talked about it and I'd nodded and pretended I was interested. True, she'd brewed me up a potion that healed my aches and pains, but I preferred the safety of something I could purchase at a drug store.

The idea of me cooking up something that another person might drink gave me cold shivers just thinking of everything that could go wrong. I'd looked at some recipes in my grimoire. It wasn't like following a recipe in a cookbook and ending up with a Cordon Bleu worthy meal.

The ingredients in the potion I'd read included bloodroot, mugwort and nettles. I knew the resulting brew would look like sewer effluent and probably taste worse.

Vi looked altogether too excited for my liking. She said, "We're going to cook up a love potion that will make Charlie fall in love with Alice." She heaved a sigh of happiness. "You'll love it. It's like matchmaking with herbs. Brewing up a happily ever after."

With my luck, instead of cooking up eternal happiness, I'd give them both a case of dysentery.

Order your copy today! *Purls and Potions* is Book 5 in the Vampire Knitting Club series.

ALSO BY NANCY WARREN

The best way to keep up with new releases, plus enjoy bonus content and prizes is to join Nancy's newsletter at nancywarren.net

Vampire Knitting Club

Tangles and Treasons - a free prequel for Nancy's newsletter subscribers

The Vampire Knitting Club - Book 1

Stitches and Witches - Book 2

Crochet and Cauldrons - Book 3

Stockings and Spells - Book 4

Purls and Potions - Book 5

Fair Isle and Fortunes - Book 6

Lace and Lies - Book 7

Bobbles and Broomsticks - Book 8

Popcorn and Poltergeists - Book 9

Garters and Gargoyles - Book 10

Cat's Paws and Curses a Holiday Whodunnit

The Great Witches Baking Show

The Great Witches Baking Show - Book 1

Baker's Coven - Book 2

A Rolling Scone - Book 3

Toni Diamond Mysteries

Toni is a successful saleswoman for Lady Bianca Cosmetics in this series of humorous cozy mysteries. Along with having an eye for beauty and a head for business, Toni's got a nose for trouble and she's never shy about following her instincts, even when they lead to murder.

Frosted Shadow - Book 1

Ultimate Concealer - Book 2

Midnight Shimmer - Book 3

A Diamond Choker For Christmas - A Toni Diamond Mysteries Novella

The Almost Wives Club

An enchanted wedding dress is a matchmaker in this series of romantic comedies where five runaway brides find out who the best men really are!

The Almost Wives Club: Kate - Book 1

Second Hand Bride - Book 2

Bridesmaid for Hire - Book 3

The Wedding Flight - Book 4

If the Dress Fits - Book 5

Take a Chance series

Meet the Chance family, a cobbled together family of eleven kids who are all grown up and finding their ways in life and love.

Kiss a Girl in the Rain - Book 1

For a complete list of books, check out Nancy's website at nancywarren.net

ABOUT THE AUTHOR

Nancy Warren is the USA Today Bestselling author of more than 70 novels. She's originally from Vancouver, Canada, though she tends to wander and has lived in England, Italy and California at various times. While living in Oxford she dreamed up The Vampire Knitting Club. She's currently in Bath, UK, where she often pretends she's Jane Austen. Or at least a character in a Jane Austen novel. Favorite moments include being the answer to a crossword puzzle clue in Canada's National Post newspaper, being featured on the front page of the New York Times when her book Speed Dating launched Harlequin's NASCAR series, and being nominated three times for Romance Writers of America's RITA award. She has an MA in Creative Writing from Bath Spa University. She's an avid hiker, loves chocolate and most of all, loves to hear from readers! The best way to stay in touch is to sign up for Nancy's newsletter at www.nancywarren.net. Or in her private FaceBook group www.facebook.com/groups/Nancy-WarrenKnitwits

To learn more about Nancy and her books
www.nancywarren.net

9 781928 145554